Lost on Venus

EDGAR RICE BURROUGHS

NEW ENGLISH LIBRARY
TIMES MIRROR

First published in the United States of America by Canaveral Press Ltd., in 1963

*

FIRST FOUR SQUARE EDITION 1965
An NEL edition April 1971
New NEL edition April 1973
This new edition, December 1974

*

NEL Books are published by The New English Library Limited, from Barnard's Inn, Holborn, London, E.C.1. Made and printed in Great Britain by C. Nicholls & Company Ltd.

4500 22277

FOREWORD

WHEN Carson Napier left my office to fly to Guadalupe Island and take off for Mars in the giant rocket that he had constructed there for that purpose, I was positive that I should never see him again in the flesh. That his highly developed telepathic powers, through the medium of which he hoped to communicate with me, might permit me to envisage him and communicate with him I had no doubts; but I expected no messages after he had detonated the first rocket. I though that Carson Napier would die within a few seconds of the initiation of his mad scheme.

But my fears were not realized. I followed him through his mad, month-long journey through space, trembling with him as the gravitation of the Moon drew the great rocket from its course and sent it hurtling toward the Sun, holding my breath as he was gripped by the power of Venus, and thrilling to his initial adventures upon that mysterious, cloud-enwrapped planet – Amtor, as it is known to its human inhabitants.

His love for the unattainable Duare, daughter of a king, their capture by the cruel Thorians, his self-sacrificing rescue of the girl, held me enthralled.

I saw the strange, unearthly birdman bearing Duare from the rockbound shore of Noobol to the ship that was to bear her back to her native land just as Carson Napier was overwhelmed and made prisoner by a strong band of Thorians.

I saw – but now let Carson Napier tell his own story in his own words while I retire again to the impersonality of my rôle of amanuensis.

CHAPTER 1

The Seven Doors

Leading my captors, but taking no part in the capture, were Moosko, the ongyan, and Vilor, the Thorist spy, who had together conceived and carried out the abduction of Duare from her quarters aboard the Sofal.

After they had reached the mainland, carried there by the klangan, those strange winged humans of Venus, they left Duare to her fate when the party was attacked by the hairy wild men from whom I had fortunately been able to rescue her with the aid of the angan who had so heroically defended her.

But now, though they had abandoned her to almost certain death, they were furious with me for having caused her to be carried from their clutches back to the deck of the Sofal by the last survivor of the klangan; and having me within their power, after some one else had disarmed me, they became courageous again and attacked me violently.

I think they would have killed me on the spot had not a better idea suggested itself to another member of the Thorist party that had captured me.

Vilor, who had been unarmed, seized a sword from one of his fellows and set upon me with the evident intention of hacking me to pieces, when this man intervened.

'Wait!' he cried. 'What has this man done that he should be killed swiftly and without suffering?'

'What do you mean!' demanded Vilor, lowering the point of his weapon.

This country in which we were was almost as strange to Vilor as to me, for he was from the distant mainland of Thora proper, while the party that had assisted in my capture were natives of this land of Noobol who had been induced to join the Thorists in their world-wide attempt to foment discord and overthrow all established forms of government and replace them with their own oligarchy of ignorance.

As Vilor hesitated, the other explained. 'In Kapdor', he

said, 'we have far more interesting ways of disposing of enemies than spitting them on a sword.'

'Explain,' commanded the ongyan, Moosko. 'This man does not deserve the mercy of a quick death. A prisoner aboard the Sofal, with other Vepajans, he led a mutiny in which all the ship's officers were murdered; then he seized the Sovang, liberated her prisoners, looted her, threw her big guns into the sea, and sailed away upon a piratical expedition.

'In the Sofal, he overhauled the Yan, a merchant ship on which I, an ongyan, was a passenger. Ignoring my authority, he opened fire upon the Yan and then boarded her. After looting her and destroying her armament, he took me prisoner aboard the Sofal. He treated me with the utmost disrespect, threatening my life and destroying my liberty.

'For these things he must die, and if you have a death commensurate with his crimes, you shall not go unrewarded by those who rule Thora.'

'Let us take him back to Kapdor with us,' said the man. 'There we have the room with seven doors, and I promise you that if he be an intelligent being, he will suffer more agony within its circular walls than any prick of a sword point might inflict upon him.'

'Good!' exclaimed Vilor, handing his sword back to the man from whom he had borrowed it. 'The creature deserves the worst.'

They led me back along the coast in the direction from which they had come, and during the march I discovered from their conversation among themselves to what unfortunate chance I could attribute the ill fortune that had befallen me at the very moment when it seemed possible that Duare and I might easily return to the Sofal and our loyal friends.

This armed party from Kapdor had been searching for an escaped prisoner when their attention had been attracted by the fight between the hairy wild men and the klangans who were defending Duare, just as I had similarly been attracted to the scene while searching for the beautiful daughter of Mintep, the jong of Vepaja.

As they were coming to investigate, they met Moosko and Vilor fleeing from the engagement, and these two had accompanied them back to the scene just as Duare, the remaining angan, and I had sighted the Sofal off shore and were planning on signalling to her.

As the birdman could transport but one of us at a time, I had commanded him, much against his will, to carry Duare to the ship. She refused to desert me, and the angan feared to return to the Sofal from which he had aided in the abduction of the princess; but I at length compelled him to seize Duare and fly away with her just as the party of Thorists were upon us.

There had been a stiff gale blowing from the sea; and I was much worried for fear that the angan might not have been able to beat his way against it to the deck of the Sofal, but I had known that death beneath the waters of the sea would be far less horrible to Duare than captivity among the Thorists and especially in the power of Moosko.

My captors had watched the birdman, battling his way against the gale with his burden, but only for a few minutes; then they had started upon the return march to Kapdor when Moosko had suggested that Kamlot, who was now in command of the Sofal, would doubtless land a force and pursue them as soon as Duare acquainted him with the fact of my capture. And so, as our path dropped behind the rocky pinnacles of the shore line, the angan and Duare were lost to our view; and I felt that I was doomed to go through whatever brief hours of life remained to me without knowledge of the fate of the gorgeous Venusan girl whom fate had decreed should be my first love.

The fact that I should have chanced to fall in love with this particular girl, in the land of Vepaja where there were so many beautiful girls, was in itself a tragedy. She was the virgin daughter of a jong, or king, whom custom rendered sacrosanct.

During the eighteen years of her life she had been permitted to see nor speak to no man other than members of the royal family and a few trusted servitors until I had invaded her garden and forced my unwelcome attentions upon her. And then shortly thereafter, the worst had befallen her. A raiding party of Thorists had succeeded in abducting her, members of the same party that had captured Kamlot and me.

She had been shocked and terrified at my avowal of my

love, but she had not informed against me. She had seemed to despise me up until the last moment upon the summit of the rocky cliffs overlooking the raging Venusan sea, when I had ordered the angan to carry her to the Sofal; then, with outstretched hands, she had implored, 'Do not send me away from you, Carson! Do not send me away! I love you!'

Those words, those unbelievable words, still rang in my ears, leaving me elated even in the face of the nameless death that I knew awaited me in the mysterious chamber of seven doors that they mentioned.

The Thorists from Kapdor who formed my escort were much intrigued by my blond hair and blue eyes, for such were unknown to any of the Venusans I had yet encountered. They questioned Vilot concerning me; but he insisted that I was a Vepajan, and as the Vepajans are the deadliest enemies of the Thorists, he could not more effectually have sealed my doom even had I not been guilty of the offenses charged against me by Moosko.

'He says that he comes from another world far from Amtor; but he was captured in Vepaja in company with another Vepajan, and he was well known to Duare, the daughter of Mintep, the jong of Vepaja.'

'What other world could there be but Amtor?' scoffed one of the soldiers.

'None, of course,' assented another; 'beyond Amtor lie only boiling rocks and fire.'

The cosmic theory of the Amtorians is as circumscribed by impenetrable fog as is their world by the two great cloud envelopes that surround it. From the spouting lava of their volcanoes they visualize a sea of molten rock upon which floats Amtor, a vast disc; the occasional rents in the enveloping clouds, through which they glimpse the fiery sun and feel his consuming heat, assure them that all is fire above; and when these rents occur at night, they believe the myriad stars to be sparks from the eternal, fiery furnace that fuses the molten sea beneath their world.

I was almost exhausted by what I had passed through since the screeching of the hurricane and the plunging of the Sofal had awakened me the preceding night. After the great wave had swept me overboard, I had had a battle with the great waves that would have wholly sapped the strength of a less powerful man than I; and then, after I had reached shore, I had walked far in search of Duare and her abductors only to have my strength further sapped by a strenuous battle with the savage kloonobargan, the hairy beast-men who had attacked her abductors.

And now I was about all in as, topping a rise, there burst upon my view a walled city lying close to the sea at the mouth of a little valley. I guessed that this was Kapdor, our destination; and though I knew that death awaited me there, I could not but look forward to the city with anticipation, since I guessed that food and drink might also await me behind those substantial walls.

The city gate through which we entered was well guarded, suggesting that Kapdor had many enemies; and all the citizens were armed – with swords, or daggers, or pistols. The last were similar to those I had first become acquainted with in the house of Duran, the father of Kamlot, in the tree-city of Kooaad, which is the capital of Mintep's island kingdom, Vepaja.

These weapons discharge the lethal r-ray, which destroys animal tissue, and are far more deadly than the .45 automatics with which we are familiar, since they discharge a continuous stream of the destructive rays as long as the mechanism which generates them is kept in action by the pressure of a finger.

There were many people on the streets of Kapdor, but they seemed dull and apathetic. Even the sight of a blond-haired, blue-eyed prisoner aroused no interest within their sodden brains. To me they appeared like beasts of burden, performing their dull tasks without the stimulous of imagination or of hope. It was these that were armed with daggers, and there was another class that I took to be the soldier class who carried swords and pistols. These seemed more alert and cheerful, for evidently they were a more favored class, but they had no appearance of being any more intelligent than the others.

The buildings for the most part were mean hovels of a single story, but there were others that were more pretentious – two and even three story buildings. Many were of lumber, for forests are plentiful in this portion of Amtor, though I had seen none of the enormous trees such as grow upon the island of Vepaja and which afforded me my first introduction to Venus.

There were a number of stone buildings facing the streets along which I was conducted; but they were all box-like, unprepossessing structures with no hint of artistic or imaginative genius. In that respect they were reminiscent of the so-called modern architecture that was just making itself felt before I left earth.

Presently my captors led me into an open square surrounded by larger if not more beautiful buildings than we had previously passed. Yet even here were squalor and indications of inefficiency and incompetence.

I was led into a building the entrance to which was guarded by soldiers. Vilor, Moosko, and the leader of the party that had captured me accompanied me into the interior, where, in a bare room, a large gross-appearing man was asleep in a chair with his feet on a table that evidently served him both as desk and dining table, for its top was littered with papers and the remains of a meal.

Disturbed by our entrance, the sleeper opened his eyes and blinked dully at us for a moment.

'Greetings, Friend Sov!' exclaimed the officer who accompanied me.

'Oh, it is you, Friend Hokal?' mumbled Sov, sleepily. 'And who are these others?'

'The Ongyan Moosko from Thora, Vilor, another Friend, and a Vepajan prisoner I captured.'

At the mention of Moosko's title, Sov arose, for an ongyan is one of the oligarchy and a great man. 'Greetings, Ongyan Moosko!' he cried. 'So you have brought us a Vepajan! Is he a doctor, by chance?'

'I do not know and I do not care,' snapped Moosko. 'He is a cutthroat and a scoundrel; and, doctor or no doctor, he dies.'

'But we need doctors badly,' insisted Sov. 'We are dying of disease and old age. If we do not have a doctor soon, we shall be dead.'

'You heard what I said, did you not, Friend Sov?' demanded Moosko testily.

'Yes, Ongyan,' replied the officer, meekly; 'he shall die. Shall I have him destroyed at once?'

'Friend Hokal tells me that you have a slower and pleasanter way of dispatching villains than by gun or sword. I am interested. Tell me about it.'

'I referred to the room of the seven doors,' explained Hokal. 'You see, this man's offenses were great; he made the great Ongyan a prisoner and even threatened his life.'

'We have no death adequate to such a crime,' cried the horrified Sov; 'but the room of the seven doors, which is the best that we have to offer, shall be made ready.'

'Describe it, describe it,' snapped Moosko. 'What is it like? What will happen to him? How will he die?'

'Let us not explain it in the presence of the prisoner,' said Hokal, 'if you would reap the full pleasure of the room of the seven doors.'

'Yes, lock him up; lock him up!' ordered Moosko. 'Put him in a cell.'

Sov summoned a couple of soldiers, who conducted me to a rear room and showed me down into a dark, windowless cellar. They slammed down and locked the heavy trap door above me and left me to my gloomy thoughts.

The room of the seven doors! The title intrigued me. I wondered what awaited me there, what strange form of horrible death. Perhaps it might not be so terrible after all; perhaps they were attempting to make my end more terrible by suggestion.

So this was to be the termination of my mad attempt to reach Mars! I was to die alone in this far flung outpost of the Thorists in the land of Noobol that was scarcely more than a name to me. And there was so much to see upon Venus, and I had seen so little.

I recalled all that Danus had told me, the things concerning Venus that had so stimulated my imagination – sketchy tales, little more than fables, of Karbol, the cold country, where roamed strange and savage beasts and even more strange and more savage men; and Trabol, the warm country, where lay the island of Vepaja toward which chance had guided the rocket in which I had journeyed from earth. Most of all had I been interested in Strabol, the hot country, for I was positive that this corresponded with the equatorial regions of the planet, and that beyond it lay a vast, unexplored region entirely unguessed of by the inhabitants of the southern hemisphere – the north temperate zone.

One of my hopes when I seized the Sofal and set myself up as a pirate chieftain was that I might find an ocean passage north to this *terra incognita.* What strange races, what new civilizations might I not discover there! But now I had reached the end, not only of hope but of life as well.

I determined to stop thinking about it. It was going to be too easy to feel sorry for myself if I were to keep on in that vein, and that would never do; it unnerves a man.

I had enough pleasant memories stored away inside my head, and these I called to my aid. The happy days that I had spent in India before my English father died were food for glorious recollection. I though of old Chand Kabi, my tutor, and of all that I had learned from him outside of school books; not the least of which was that satisfying philosophy which I found it expedient to summon to my aid in this, my last extremity. It was Chand Kabi who had taught me to use my mind to the fullest extent of its resources and to project it across illimitable space to another mind attuned to receive its messages, without which power the fruits of my strange adventure must die with me in the room of the seven doors.

I had other pleasant recollections to dissolve the gloom that shrouded my immediate future; they were of the good and loyal friends I had made during my brief sojourn on this distant planet: Kamlot, my best friend on Venus, and those 'three musketeers' of the Sofal Gamfor, the farmer; Kiron, the soldier; and Zog, the slave. These had been friends indeed!

And then, pleasantest memory of all, there was Duare. She was worth all that I had risked; her last words to me compensated even for death. She had told me that she loved me – she, the incomparable, the unattainable – she, the hope of a world, the daughter of a king. I could scarcely believe that my ears had not tricked me, for always before, in the few words she had deigned to fling me, she had sought to impress upon me the fact that not only was she not for such as I but that she abhorred me. Women are peculiar – as peculiar upon Venus as upon earth.

How long I remained in that dark hole, I do not know. It must have been several hours; but at last I heard footsteps in the room above, and then the trap door was raised and I was ordered to come up.

Several soldiers awaiting me escorted me back to the filthy office of Sov, where I found that officer seated in conversation with Moosko, Vilor, and Hokal. A jug and glasses, together with the fumes of strong drink, attested the manner in which they had enlivened their conference.

'Take him to the room of the seven doors,' Sov directed the soldiers who guarded me; and as I was escorted into the open square, the four who had condemned me to death followed.

A short distance from Sov's office, the soldiers turned into a narrow, crooked alley; and presently we came to a large open space in the center of which were several buildings, one a circular tower rising above the others from the center of a large enclosure that was surrounded by a high stone wall.

Through a small gate we passed into a covered passageway, a gloomy tunnel, at the end of which was a stout door which one of the soldiers opened with a great key that Hokal passed to him; then the soldiers stood aside, and I entered the room, followed by Sov, Moosko, Vilor, and Hokal.

I found myself in a circular apartment in the walls of which were seven identical doors placed at regular intervals about the circumference; so that there was no way of distinguishing one door from another.

In the center of the room was a circular table upon which were seven vessels containing seven varieties of food and seven jugs containing liquids. Depending above the center of the table was a rope with a noose in the end of it, the upper end of the rope being lost in the shadows of the high ceiling, for the chamber was but dimly lighted.

Suffering with thirst, as I was, and being half famished for food, the sight of that laden table aroused my flagging spirits. It was evident that even if I were about to die I should not die hungry. The Thorists might be cruel and heartless in some respects, but it was clear that there was some kindliness in them, else they would never furnish such an abundance of food to a condemned man.

'Attend!' snapped Sov, addressing me. 'Listen well to what I shall say to you.' Moosko was inspecting the room with a gloating smile on his thick lips. 'We shall leave you here alone presently,' continued Sov. 'If you can escape from this building, your life will be spared. As you see, there are seven doors leading from this room; none of them has bolt or bar. Beyond each is a corridor identical to that through which we just approached the chamber. You are free to open any of the doors and enter any of these corridors. After you pass through a door, a spring will close it; and you cannot open it again from the opposite side, the doors being so constructed that there is nothing to lay hold upon wherewith to open them, with the exception of that one which let us into the room; through that one door lies life; beyond the others, death.

'In the corridor of the second door you will step upon a hidden spring that will cause long, sharp spikes to be released upon you from all directions; and upon these you will be impaled and die.

'In the third corridor a similar spring will ignite a gas that will consume you in flames. In the fourth, r-rays will be loosed upon you, and you will die instantly. In the fifth, another door will open at the far end and admit a tharban.'

'What is a tharban?' I asked.

Sov looked at me in astonishment. 'You know as well as I,' he growled.

'I have told you that I am from another world,' I snapped. 'I do not know what the word means.'

'It will do no harm to tell him,' suggested Vilor; 'for if, by chance, he does not know, some of the horror of the room of the seven doors may be lost upon him.'

'Not a bad thought,' interjected Moosko. 'Describe the tharban, Friend Sov.'

'It is a terrible beast,' explained Sov, 'a huge and terrible beast. It is covered with stiff hair, like bristles, and is of a reddish color with white stripes running lengthwise of its body, its belly being of a bluish tinge. It has great jaws and terrible talons, and it eats naught but flesh.'

At that instant a terrific roar that seemed to shake the building broke upon our ears.

'That is the tharban,' said Hokal with a grin. 'He has not eaten for three days, and he is not only very hungry but he is very angry.'

"And what lies beyond the sixth door?' I demanded.

'In the corridor beyond the sixth door hidden jets will deluge you with corrosive acid. It will fill your eyes and burn them out; and it will consume your flesh slowly, but you will not die too quickly. You will have ample time in which to repent the crimes that brought you to the room of the seven doors. The sixth door, I think, is the most terrible of all.'

'To my mind the seventh is worse,' remarked Hokal.

'Perhaps,' admitted Sov. 'In the seventh, death is longer in coming, and the mental agony is protracted. When you step upon the concealed spring in the corridor beyond the seventh door, the walls commence to move slowly toward you. Their movement is so slow as to be almost imperceptible, but eventually they will reach you and slowly crush you between them.'

"And what is the purpose of the noose above the table?' I asked.

'In the agony of indecision as to which door is the door to life,' explained Sov, 'you will be tempted to destroy yourself, and the noose is there for that purpose. But it is cunningly arranged at such a distance above the table that you cannot utilize it in such a way as to break your neck and bring death quickly; you can only strangle to death.'

'It appears to me that you have gone to considerable pains to destroy your enemies,' I suggested.

'The room of the seven doors was not designed primarily to inflict death,' explained Sov. 'It is used as a means for converting unbelievers to Thorism, and you would be surprised to know how efficacious it has been,' he added, with a laugh.

'I can imagine,' I replied. 'And now that you have told me the worst, may I be permitted to satisfy my hunger and thirst before I die?'

'All within this room are yours to do with as you please during your last hours on earth, but before you eat let me explain that of the seven varieties of food upon this table one is poisoned. Before you satisfy your thirst, you may be interested in knowing that of the seven delicious beverages sparkling in those seven containers, six are poisoned. And now, murderer, we leave you. For the last time in life you are looking upon fellow human beings.'

'If life held only the hope of continuing to look upon you, I would gladly embrace death,' I replied.

In single file they left the room by the door to life. I kept my eyes upon that door to mark it well; and then the dim light went out and the room was plunged into darkness.

Quickly I crossed the chamber in a straight line toward

the exact spot where I knew the door to be, for I had been standing facing it squarely. I smiled to myself to think how simple they were to imagine that I should instantly lose my bearings because the light had been extinguished. If they had not been lying to me, I should be out of that room almost as soon as they to claim the life they had promised me.

With outstretched hands I approached the door. I felt a little dizzy, unaccountably. I was having difficulty in keeping my balance. My fingers came in contact with a moving surface; it was the wall passing across my hands toward the left. I felt a door brush past them and then another and another; then I guessed the truth – the floor upon which I stood was revolving. I had lost the door to life.

CHAPTER 2

Lost

As I stood there, plunged for the moment into despondency, the light came on again; and I saw the wall and the procession of doors passing slowly before me. Which was the door to life?

I felt very tired and rather hopeless; the pangs of hunger and thirst assailed me. I walked to the table in the center of the room. Wines and milk and water mocked me from the seven jugs. One of the seven was harmless and would quickly satisfy the gnawing craving for drink that was becoming almost torture. I examined the contents of each receptacle, testing each with my nose. There were two jugs of water, the contents of one of which had a cloudy appearance; I was positive that the other was the one unpoisoned liquid.

I lifted it in my hands. My parched throat begged for one little drink. I raised the jug to my lips, and then doubts assailed me. While there was a single remote chance for life I must not risk death. Resolutely I replaced the jug upon the table.

Glancing about the room, I saw a chair and a couch in the shadows against the wall beyond the table; at least, if I could not eat nor drink, I could rest and, perhaps, sleep. I would rob my captors of the fulfillment of their expectations as long as possible, and with this idea in mind I approached the couch.

The light in the room was poor, but as I was about to throw myself upon the couch it was sufficient to enable me to discern that its bed was composed of needle-sharp metal spikes, and my vision of restful sleep was dispelled. An examination of the chair revealed the fact that it was similarly barbed.

What ingenious fiendishness the Thorists had displayed in the conception of this room and its appurtenances! There was nothing about it that I might use that was not feral, with the single exception of the floor; and I was so tired as I stretched myself at full length upon it that for the moment it seemed a luxurious couch.

It is true that the discomfort of its hardness became more and more appreciable; yet, so exhausted was I, I was upon the verge of sleep, half dozing, when I felt something touch my naked back – something cold and clammy.

Instantly apprehending some new and devilish form of torture, I sprang to my feet. Upon the floor, wriggling and writhing toward me, were snakes of all kinds and sizes, many of them unearthly reptiles of horrifying appearance – snakes with saber-like fangs, snakes with horns, snakes with ears, snakes of blue, of red, of green, of white, of purple. They were coming from holes near the bottom of the wall, spreading out across the floor as though they were seeking what they might devour – seeking me.

Now even the floor, that I had considered my sole remaining hope, was denied me. I sprang to the table top amidst the poisoned food and drink, and there I crouched on one knee, watching the hideous reptiles squirming about on the floor beneath.

Suddenly the food began to tempt me, but now for a reason apart from hunger. I saw in it escape from the hopelessness and torture of my situation. What chance had I for life? My captors had known, when they put me in here, that I would never come out alive. What a vain and foolish thing was hope under such circumstances!

I thought of Duare; and I asked myself, what of her? Even were I to escape through some miracle, what chance had I of ever seeing Duare again? I, who could not even guess the direction in which lay Vepaja, the land of her people, the land to which Kamlot was most assuredly returning her even now.

I had harbored a half, faint-hearted hope immediately after my capture that Kamlot would land the fighting crew of the Sofal in an attempt to rescue me; but I had long since abandoned it, for I knew that his first duty was to Duare, the daughter of his king, and that no consideration would tempt him to delay an instant the return voyage to Vepaja.

As, immersed in thought, I watched the snakes, there came faintly to my ears what sounded like a woman's scream; and I wondered, indifferently, what new horror was occurring in this hateful city. Whatever it was, I could neither know nor prevent; and so it made little impression upon me, especially in view of a sudden, new interest in the snakes.

One of the larger of them, a great, hideous creature some twenty feet in length, had raised his head to the level of the table and was watching me with its lidless, staring eyes. It seemed to me that I could almost read that dim, reptilian brain reacting to the presence of food.

It laid its head flat upon the table; and, its body undulating slowly, it glided toward me across the table top.

I glanced quickly about the room, vainly seeking some avenue of escape. There, evenly spaced in the periphery of the chamber, were the seven doors, stationary now; for the floor had ceased to revolve shortly after the light had come on again. Behind one of those identical doors lay life; behind each of the other six, death. Upon the floor, between them and me, were the snakes. They had not distributed themslves evenly over the entire area of the flagging. There were spaces across which one might run swiftly without encountering more than an occasional reptile; yet a single one, were it venomous, would be fatal as a score of them; and I was harassed by knowledge of my ignorance of the nature of a single one of the numerous species represented.

The hideous head of the serpent that had raised itself to the table top was gliding slowly toward me; the greater part of its length extended along the floor, moved in undulating waves as it crept after the head. As yet it had given no indication of the method of its attack. I did not know if it might be expected to strike first with poison fangs, to crush within its constricting folds, or merely to seize in widespread jaws and swallow as I had seen snakes, in my boyhood, swallowing frogs and birds. In any event the outlook was far from pleasing.

I shot a quick glance toward the doors. Should I risk all on a single cast of the die with Fate?

The repulsive head was moving closer and closer to me; I turned away from it, determined to run for the door the way to which was clearest of snakes. As I glanced quickly about the room, I saw a comparatively open avenue leading toward a door just beyond the spiked couch and chair.

One door was as good as another – I had one chance in seven! and there was no other way to differentiate one door from another. Life might lie behind this door, or death.

Here was, at least, a chance. To remain where I was, the certain prey of that hideous reptile, offered no chance whatever.

I have always enjoyed more than my share of the lucky 'breaks' of life, and now something seemed to tell me that Fate was driving me toward the one door beyond which lay life and liberty. So it was with the optimism of almost assured success that I leaped from the table and the yawning jaws of the great snake and ran toward that fateful door.

Yet I was not unmindful of that sound advice, 'Put your trust in God, my boys; and keep your powder dry!' In this event I might have paraphrased it to read, 'Put your trust in Fate, but keep an avenue of retreat open!'

I knew that the doors swung outward from the circular room and that once I had passed through one of them and it had closed behind me, there could be no returning. But how could I circumvent this?

All this that I take so long to tell occupied but a few seconds. I ran swiftly across the room, eluding the one or two snakes that were in my path; but I could not be unaware of the hissing and screaming that rose about me nor fail to see the snakes writhing and wriggling forward to intercept or pursue me.

What prompted me to seize the spiked chair as I passed it I do not know – the idea seemed to come to me like an inspiration. Perhaps, subconsciously, I hoped to use it as a weapon of defense; but it was not thus that it was to serve me.

As the nearer snakes were closing upon me I reached the door. There was no time now for further deliberation. I pushed the door open and stepped into the gloomy corridor beyond! It was exactly like the corridor through which I had been brought to the room of the seven doors. Hope sprang high within my breast, but I braced the door open with the spiked chair – I was keeping my powder dry!

I had taken but a few steps beyond the doorway when my blood was frozen by the most terrifying roar that I have ever heard, and in the gloom ahead I saw two blazing balls of fire. I had opened the door to the fifth corridor that led to the lair of the tharban!

I did not hesitate. I *knew* that death awaited me in the darkness of that gloomy hole. No, it was not awaiting me;

it was coming charging toward me. I turned and fled for the temporary safety that the light and space of the larger room would give me, and as I passed through the doorway I sought to snatch the chair away and let the door close in the face of the savage beast that was pursuing me. But something went wrong. The door, impelled by a powerful spring, closed too quickly – before I could drag the chair out of the way, wedging it tightly so that I could not free it; and there it stuck, holding the door half open.

I had been in tight places before, but nothing like this. Before me were the snakes and, dominating them, the huge creature that had sought me on the table; behind me was the roaring tharban. And now the only haven that I could think of was that very table top from which I had so thankfully escaped a few seconds before.

To the right of the doorway was a small open space in which there were no snakes; and, hurdling those hissing and striking at me upon the threshold, I leaped to it at the very instant that the tharban sprang into the room.

For the instant I was held in the power of a single urge – to reach the top of the table. How futile and foolish the idea may have been did not occur to me; my mind clung to it to the effacement of all other thoughts. And perhaps because of my singleness of purpose I would have reached my goal in any event, but when I stood again among the dishes and decanters of poisoned food and drink and turned to face my fate, I saw that another factor had intervened to save me for the moment and permit me to attain the questionable sanctuary of the table top.

Halfway between the door and the table the tharban, a fighting, rearing, roaring monster, was being set upon by the snakes. He snapped and struck and clawed, ripping them to pieces, tearing them in halves; but still they came for him, hissing, striking, entwining. Bodies cut in two, heads severed still sought to reach him; and from all parts of the room came ten to replace each that he disposed of.

Immense and threatening, standing out above them all, rose the huge reptile that had sought to devour me; and the tharban seemed to realize that in this creature lay a foe worthy of its mettle; for while he brushed away the lesser snakes with irritable contempt, he always faced the great one and launched his most vicious attacks against it. But of what avail! With lightning-like movements the sinuous coils darted hither and thither, eluding every blow like some practiced boxer and striking with terrific force at every opening, burying its fangs deep in the bloody flesh of the tharban.

The roars and screams of the carnivore mingled with the screams and hisses of the reptiles to produce the most horrid din that the mind of man might imagine, or at least so it seemed to me, cooped up in this awful room filled with implacable engines of death.

Which would win this struggle of the Titans? What difference could it make to me other than the difference as to which belly I should eventually fill! Yet I could not help watching the encounter with the excited interest of a disinterested spectator at some test of strength and skill.

It was a bloody encounter, but the blood was all that of the tharban and the lesser snakes. The huge creature that was championing my cause that it might later devour me was so far unscathed. How it manipulated its huge body with sufficient quickness to avoid the savage rushes of the tharban is quite beyond me, though perhaps an explanation lies in the fact that it usually met a charge with a terrific blow of its head that sent the tharban reeling back half stunned and with a new wound.

Presently the tharban ceased its offensive and commenced to back away. I watched the weaving, undulating head of the great snake following every move of its antagonist. The lesser snakes swarmed over the body of the tharban; it seemed not to notice them. Then, suddenly, it wheeled and sprang for the entrance to the corridor that led to its lair.

This, evidently, was the very thing for which the snake had been waiting. It lay half coiled where it had been fighting; and now like a giant spring suddenly released it shot through the air; and, so quickly that I could scarcely perceive the action, it wrapped a dozen coils about the body of the tharban, raised its gaping jaws above the back of the beast's neck, and struck!

A horrid scream burst from the distended jaws of the stricken carnivore as the coils tightened suddenly about it. I heard bones cracking and crushing, as blood squirted in streams from the burst body.

I breathed a sigh of relief as I thought for how long an entire tharban might satisfy the hunger of this twenty-foot snake and distract its mind from other sources of food supply, and as I anticipated this respite, the mighty victor unwound its coils from about the body of its victim and turned its head slowly in my direction.

I gazed spellbound for a moment into those cold, lidless eyes and then horror-stricken as I saw the creature gliding slowly toward the table. It did not move swiftly as in battle but very slowly. There was seemingly predetermined finality, an inevitableness, in that undulating approach that was almost paralyzing in its frightfulness.

I saw it raise its head to the level of the table top; I saw the head glide among the dishes toward me. I could stand it no longer. I turned to run – where made no difference – anywhere, if only the length of the room, to get away even for a moment from the cold glitter of those baleful eyes. As I turned, two things happened: I heard again, faintly, the screams of a woman; and my face struck the noose dangling from the dense shadows of the rafters.

The screams made little impression upon me, but the noose gave birth to a new thought – not the thought that it was placed there to arouse but another. It suggested an avenue of escape from the snakes; nor was I long in availing myself of it.

I felt the snout of the snake touch my bare leg as I sprang upward and seized the rope above the noose; I heard a loud hiss of rage as I clambered, hand over hand, toward the gloomy shadows where I hoped to find at least temporary refuge.

The upper end of the rope was fastened to a metal eyebolt set in a great beam. Onto this beam I clambered and looked down. The mighty serpent was hissing and writhing below me. He had raised a third of his body upward and was endeavoring to coil about the dangling rope and follow me upward, but it swung away and eluded his efforts.

I doubted that a snake of his great girth could ascend this relatively tiny strand; but, not caring to take the chance, I drew the rope up and looped it over the beam. For the moment at least, I was safe; and I breathed a deep sigh of relief. Then I commenced to look about me.

The shadows were dense and almost impenetrable, yet it

appeared that the ceiling of the room was still far above me; about me was a maze of beams and braces and trusses. I determined to explore this upper region of the room of the seven doors. Standing upright upon the beam, I moved cautiously toward the wall. At the end of the beam I discovered a narrow walk-way that, clinging to the wall, apparently encircled the room. It was about two feet wide and had no handrail. It seemed to be something in the nature of a scaffolding left by the workmen who had constructed the building.

As I took my exploratory way along it, feeling each step carefully, and brushing the wall with my hand, I again heard the agonized scream that had twice before attracted my attention if not my keen interest; and I was still more interested in my troubles than in those of some unknown female of this alien race.

And a moment later my fingers came in contact with something that drove all thoughts of screaming women from my mind. By feel, it was the frame of a door or of a window. With both hands I examined my find. Yes, it was a door! It was a narrow door about six feet in height. I felt the hinges; I searched for a latch – and at last I found it. Cautiously I manipulated it, and presently I felt the door move toward me.

What lay beyond? Some new and fiendishly conceived form of death or torture, perhaps; perhaps freedom. I could not know without opening that portal of mystery.

I hesitated, but not for long. Slowly I drew the door toward me, an eye close to the widening crack. A breath of night air blew in upon me; I saw the faint luminosity of a Venusan night.

Could it be possible that with all their cunning the Thorists had inadvertently left this avenue of escape from this lethal chamber? I could scarcely credit it, yet there was naught that I could do but go on and chance whatever lay beyond.

I opened the door and stepped out upon a balcony which extended in both directions until it passed from the range of my visions beyond the curve of the circular wall to which it clung.

At the outer edge of the balcony was a low parapet behind which I now crouched while I reconnoitered my new situation. No new danger seemed to threaten me, yet I was still suspicious. I moved cautiously forward upon a tour of investigation, and again an agonized scream rent the silence of the night. This time it seemed quite close; previously, the walls of the building in which I had been imprisoned had muffled it.

I was already moving in the direction of the sound, and I continued to do so. I was searching for an avenue of descent to the ground below, not for a damsel in distress. I am afraid that at that moment I was callous and selfish and far from chivalric; but, if the truth be known, I would not have cared had I known that every inhabitant of Kapdor, male and female, was being destroyed.

Rounding the curve of the tower, I came in sight of another building standing but a few yards distant; and at the same instant I saw something that greatly aroused my interest and even my hope. It was a narrow causeway leading from the balcony on which I stood to a similar balcony on the adjoining structure.

Simultaneously the screams were renewed; they seemed to be coming from the interior of the building I had just discovered. It was not the screams, however, that lured me across the causeway, but the hope that I might find there the means of descent to the ground.

Crossing quickly to the other balcony, I followed it to the nearest corner; and as I rounded it I saw a light apparently shining from windows on a level with it.

At first I was of a mind to turn back lest, in passing the windows, I be discovered; but once again that scream burst upon my ears, and this time it was so close that I knew it must come from the apartment from which the light shone. There was such a note of hopelessness and fear in it that I could no longer ignore the demand it made upon my sympathies; and, setting discretion aside, I approached the window nearest me.

It was wide open, and in the room beyond I saw a women in the clutches of a man. The fellow was holding her down upon a couch and with a sharp dagger was pricking her. Whether he had it in his mind to kill her eventually or not was not apparent; his sole purpose at the moment seeming to be torture.

The fellow's back was toward me, and his body hid the

features of the woman; but when he pricked her and she screamed, he laughed – a hideous, gloating laugh. I guessed at once the psychopathic type he represented, deriving pleasure from the infliction of pain upon the object of his maniacal passion.

I saw him stoop to kiss her, and then she struck him in the face; and as she did so he half turned his head to avoid the blow, revealing his profile to me; and I saw that it was Moosko, the ongyan.

He must have partially released his hold upon her as he shrank aside, for the girl half rose from the couch in an effort to escape him. As she did so her face was revealed to me, and my blood froze in rage and horror. It was Duare!

With a single bound I cleared the sill and was upon him. Grasping him by the shoulder, I whirled him about; and when he saw my face, he voiced a cry of terror and shrank back, drawing his pistol from its holster. Instantly I closed with him, grasping the weapon and turning its muzzle toward the ceiling. He toppled backward across the couch, carrying me with him; both of us falling on top of Duare.

Moosko had dropped his dagger as he reached for his pistol, and now I tore the latter from his grasp and hurled it aside; then my fingers sought his throat.

He was a large, gross man, fat and pussy; but he was not without strength; and the fear of death seemed to increase the might of his muscles. He fought with the desperation of the doomed.

I dragged him from the couch lest Duare be injured; and we rolled upon the floor, each intent upon winning a death hold upon the other. He was screaming for help now, and I redoubled my efforts to shut off his wind before his cries attracted the aid of any of his fellows.

He was snapping at me like a savage beast even as he screamed and alternately striking at my face and seeking to close upon my throat. I was exhausted from all that I had passed through and from loss of sleep and lack of feed. I realized that I was weakening rapidly, while Moosko seemed to my frenzied imagination to be growing stronger.

I knew that if I were not to be vanquished and Duare lost, I must overcome my antagonist without further loss of time; and so, drawing away from him to get greater distance for a blow, I drove my fist full into his face with all my remaining strength.

For an instant he wilted, and in that instant my fingers closed upon his throat. He struggled and writhed and struck me terrific blows; but, dizzy and half stunned though I was, I clung to him until at last he shuddered convulsively, relaxed, and sank to the floor, while I stood over him, panting from my exertions.

If ever a man were dead, Moosko appeared so as I arose and faced Duare where, half sitting, she crouched upon the cot where she had been a silent witness to this brief duel for possession of her.

'You!' she cried. 'It cannot be!'

'It is,' I assured her.

Slowly she arose from the couch as I approached it and stood facing me as I opened my arms to press her to me.

'No!' she cried. 'Don't touch me. It is all a mistake.'

'But you told me that you loved me, and you know that I love you,' I urged.

'That is the mistake,' she said. 'I do not love you. Fear, gratitude, sympathy, nerves distraught by all that I had passed through brought strange words to my lips that were no reflection of the sentiments that abode within my heart.'

I felt suddenly cold and weary and forlorn. All hope of happiness was crushed in my breast. I turned away from her. I no longer cared what happened to me. But only for an instant did this mood possess me. No matter whether she loved me or not, my duty remained plain before me; I must get her out of Kapdor, out of the clutches of the Thorists and, if possible, return her to her father, Mintep, king of Vepaja.

I stepped to the window and listened. Moosko's cries had not attracted succor insofar as I could perceive; no one seemed to be coming. And if they had not come in response to Duare's screams, why should they be attracted by Moosko's? I realized that there was now little likelihood that any one would investigate.

I returned to the body of Moosko and removed his harness to which was attached a sword that he had had no opportunity to draw against me; then I retrieved his dagger and pistol. I now felt much better, far more efficient. It is strange what the possession of weapons will do even for one not accustomed to bearing them, and until I had come to Venus I had seldom if ever carried a lethal weapon.

I took the time now to investigate the room, on the chance that it might contain something else of use or value to us in our bid for liberty. It was a rather large room. An attempt had been made to furnish it ornately, but the result was a monument to bad taste. It was atrocious.

At one end, however, was something that attracted my keenest interest and unqualified approval; it was a table laden with food.

I turned to Duare. 'I am going to try to take you away from Noobol,' I told her. 'I shall try also to return you to Vepaja. I may not succeed, but I shall do my best. Will you trust me and come with me?'

'How can you doubt it?' she replied. 'If you succeed in returning me to Vepaja, you will be well repaid by the honors and rewards that will be heaped upon you if my wishes prevail.'

That speech angered me, and I turned upon her with bitter words on my lips; but I did not utter them. What was the use! I once more focussed my attention upon the table. 'What I started to say,' I continued, 'is that I shall try to save you, but I can't do it on an empty stomach. I am going to eat before we leave this room. Do you care to join me?'

'We shall need strength,' she replied. 'I am not hungry, but it is wiser that we both eat. Moosko ordered the food for me, but I could not eat it while he was present.'

'Then I am not quite so objectionable as Moosko?' I inquired sarcastically.

She surveyed me for a moment in silence before she replied; and then she said, 'No, not quite.'

I turned away and approached the table where she joined me presently, and we ate in silence. There was an abundance of food, with water, wine, and other beverages; and I fell to upon them like a famished wolf.

I was curious to know how Duare had come to the Thorist city of Kapdor, but her cruel and incomprehensible treatment of me made me hesitate to evince any further interest in her. Yet presently I realized how childish was my attitude, and I asked her to tell me all that had happened since I had dispatched the angan with her toward the Sofal and the moment that I had discovered her in the clutches of Moosko.

'There is not much to tell,' she replied. 'You will recall how fearful the angan was of returning to the ship lest he be punished for the part he had taken in my abduction? They are very low creatures, with illy developed minds that react only to the most primitive forces of nature – self-preservation, hunger, fear.

'When we were almost above the deck of the Sofal, the angan hesitated and then turned back toward the shore. I asked him what he was doing, why he did not continue on and place me aboard the ship; and he replied that he was afraid. He said that they would kill him because he had helped to steal me.

'I promised him that I would protect him and that no harm would befall him, but he would not believe me. He replied that the Thorists, who had been his original masters, would reward him if he brought me back to them. That much he knew, but he had only my word that Kamlot would not have him killed. He doubted my authority with Kamlot.

'I pleaded and threatened but all to no purpose. The creature flew directly to this hideous city and delivered me to the Thorists. When Moosko learned that I had been brought here, he exercised his authority and claimed me as his own. The rest you know.'

'And now,' I said, 'we must find a way out of Kapdor and back to the coast. Perhaps the Sofal has not departed. It is possible that Kamlot has landed a party to search for us.'

'It will not be easy to escape from Kapdor,' Duare reminded me. 'As the angan brought me here, I saw the high walls and the sentries. What makes you hope that you can scale the one or elude the others?'

I shook my head. 'I can only try. First we must get out of this building. Do you recall any of the details of the building as you were brought through it?'

'Yes. There is a long hallway from the front of the building on the ground floor leading directly to stairs that lie at the back of the first floor. There are several rooms opening from each side of the hall. There were people in the two front rooms, but I could not see into the others as the doors were closed. It is possible that all of the rooms are occupied.

'We shall have to investigate, and if there are sounds of life below, we must wait until all are asleep. In the meantime I am going out on the balcony and see if I can discover some safer way to the ground.'

When I went to the window, I found that it had commenced to rain. I crept around the building until I could look down onto the street that passed before it. There was no sign of life there; it was likely that the rain had driven all within doors. In the distance I could dimly make out the outlines of the city wall at the end of the street. All was faintly illumined by the strange night light that is so peculiar a feature of the Amtorian scene. There was no stairway or ladder leading from the balcony to the ground. Our only avenue of descent was by way of the interior stairs.

I returned to Duare. 'Come,' I said, 'We might as well try it now as later.'

'Wait!' she exclaimed. 'I have a thought. It just occurred to me from something I overheard on board the Sofal relative to the customs of the Thorists. Moosko is an ongyan.'

'Was,' I corrected her, for I thought him dead.

'That is immaterial. The point is that he was one of the rulers of the so-called Free Land of Thora. His authority especially here, where there is no other member of the oligarchy, would be absolute. Yet he was unknown to any of the natives of Kapdor. What proof did he bring of his identity or his high position?'

'I do not know,' I admitted. 'But he must have had some credentials.'

'I believe that you will find upon the index finger of his right hand a great ring that is the badge of his office.'

'And you think that we could use this ring as authority to pass the sentries?'

'It is possible,' replied Duare.

'But not probable,' I demurred. 'Not by the wildest flight of fancy could any one mistake me for Moosko – unless my conceit flatters me.'

A faint smile touched Duare's lips. 'I am believing that it will not be necessary for you to look like him,' she explained. 'These people are very ignorant. Probably only a few of the common warriors saw Moosko when he arrived. Those same men would not be on watch now. Furthermore, it is night; and with the darkness and the rain the danger that your imposture will be discovered is minimized.'

'It is worth trying,' I agreed; and, going to the body of Moosko, I found the ring and removed it from his finger. It was too large for me, as the ongyan had gross, fat hands; but if any one was stupid enough to accept me as the ongyan he would not notice so minor a discrepancy as an ill-fitting ring.

Now Duare and I crept silently out of the chamber to the head of the stairs, where we paused, listening. All was dark below, but we heard the sound of voices, muffled, as though coming from behind a closed door. Slowly, stealthily, we descended the stairs. I felt the warmth of the girl's body as it brushed mine, and a great longing seized me to take her in my arms and crush her to me; but I only continued on down the stairway as outwardly cool and possessed as though no internal fire consumed me.

We reached the long hallway and had groped our way about half the distance to the door that opened upon the street, a feeling of optimism enveloping me, when suddenly a door at the front end of the corridor opened; and the passageway was illuminated by the light from the room beyond.

I saw a portion of the figure of a man standing in the open doorway. He had paused and was conversing with some one in the room he was about to quit. In another moment he might step into the corridor. Which way would he turn?

At my elbow was a door. Gingerly I tripped the latch and pushed the door open; the room beyond was in darkness; but whether or not it was occupied I could not know. Stepping through the doorway, I drew Duare in after me and partially closed the door again, standing close to the aperture, watching and listening.

Presently I heard the man who had been standing in the other doorway say, 'Until tomorrow, friends, and may you sleep in peace'; then the door slammed and the hallway was plunged into darkness again.

Now I heard footsteps; they were coming in our direction. Very gingerly I drew the sword of Moosko, the ongyan. On came the footsteps; they seemed to hesitate before the door behind which I waited; but perhaps it was only my imagination. They passed on; I heard them ascending the stairway.

Now a new fear assailed me. What if this man should enter the room in which lay the dead body of Moosko! He would spread the alarm. Instantly I recognised the necessity for immediate action.

'Now, Duare!' I whispered, and together we stepped into the corridor and almost ran to the front of the building.

A moment later we were in the street. The drizzle had become a downpour. Objects were indiscernible a few yards distant, and for this I was thankful.

We hastened along the street in the direction of the wall and the gate, passing no one, seeing no one. The rain increased in violence.

'What are you going to say to the sentry?' asked Duare.

'I do not know,' I replied candidly.

'He will be suspicious, for you can have no possible excuse for wishing to leave the safety of a walled city on a night like this and go out without an escort into a dangerous country where savage beasts and savage men roam at large.'

'I shall find a way,' I said, 'because I must.'

She made no reply, and we continued on toward the gate. It was not at a great distance from the house from which we had escaped, and presently we came upon it looming large before us through the falling rain.

A sentry, standing in the shelter of a niche in the wall, discovered us and demanded what we were doing abroad at this hour of such a night. He was not greatly concerned, since he did not know that it was in our minds to pass through the gateway; he merely assumed, I presume, that we were a couple of citizens passing by on our way to our home.

'Is Sov here?' I demanded.

'Sov here!' he exclaimed in astonishment. 'What would Sov be doing here on a night like this?'

'He was to meet me here at this hour,' I said. 'I instructed him to be here,'

'You instructed Sov to be here!' The fellow laughed. 'Who are you to give instructions to Sov?'

'I am the ongyan, Moosko,' I replied.

The man looked at me in astonishment. 'I do not know where Sov is,' he said, a little sullenly, I thought.

'Well, never mind,' I told him; 'he will be here presently; and in the meantime open up the gate, for we shall want to hurry on as soon as he arrives.'

'I cannot open the gate without orders from Sov,' replied the sentry.

'You refuse to obey an ongyan?' I demanded in the most ferocious tones I could command, hoping to awe him into compliance.

'I have never seen you before,' parried he; 'how do I know that you are an ongyan?'

I held out my hand with the ring of Moosko on the index finger. 'Do you know what that is?' I demanded.

He examined it closely. 'Yes, ongyan,' he said fearfully; 'I know,'

'Then open up the gate, and be quick about it,' I snapped.

'Let us wait until Sov comes,' he suggested. 'There will be time enough then.'

'There is no time to be lost, fellow. Open up, as I command. The Vepajan prisoner has just escaped, and Sov and I are going out with a party of warriors to search for him.'

Still the obstinate fellow hesitated; and then we heard a great shouting from the direction from which we had come, and I guessed that the fellow who had passed us in the corridor had discovered the dead body of Moosko and given the alarm.

We could hear men running. There was no more time to be lost.

'Here comes Sov with the searching party,' I cried. 'Throw open the gates, you fool, or it will go ill with you.' I drew my sword, intending to run the fellow through if he did not obey.

'Why open them now, ongyan?' he asked, hesitating; 'why not wait until Sov arrives?'

'It will save time if we have them open; that is why. Make haste now, and open them.'

As, finally, he turned to do my bidding, I heard the excited voices of the approaching men grow louder as they neared us. I could not see them yet for the rain, but as the gate swung open I glimpsed the oncoming figures through the murk.

Taking Duare by the arm I started through the gate. The sentry was still suspicious and wanted to stop us, but he was not sure of himself.

'Tell Sov to hurry,' I said, and before the man could bolster his courage to do his duty, Duare and I hastened into the outer darkness and were lost to his view in the rain.

It was my intention to reach the coast and follow along it until daylight, when, I hoped and prayed, we should sight the Sofal off shore and be able to contrive some means of signalling to her.

We groped our way through the darkness and the rain during all that terrible night. No sound of pursuit reached our ears, nor did we come upon the ocean.

The rain ceased about dawn; and when full daylight came we looked eagerly for the sea, but only low hills and rolling country dotted with trees and a distant forest where we had thought the sea to be rewarded our straining eyes.

'Where is the sea?' asked Duare.

'I do not know,' I admitted.

Only at sunrise and at sunset, for a few minutes, is it possible to differentiate between the points of the compass on Venus; then is the direction of the sun faintly indicated by a slightly intensified light along the eastern or the western horizon.

And now the sun was rising at our left, when it should have been upon our right were we going in the direction that I believed the ocean to be.

My heart sank in my breast, for I knew that we were lost.

CHAPTER 3

CANNIBALS

DUARE, who had been watching my face intently, must have read the truth in the despair of my expression.

'You do not know where the sea lies?' she asked.

I shook my head. 'No.'

'Then we are lost?'

'I am afraid so. I am sorry, Duare; I was so sure that we should find the Sofal and that you would soon be out of danger. It is all my fault, the fault of my stupidity and ignorance.'

'Do not say that; no one could have known the direction he was going during the darkness of last night. Perhaps we shall find the sea yet.'

'Even if we could, I am afraid that it will be too late to insure your safety.'

'What do you mean – that the Sofal will be gone?' she asked.

'There is that danger, of course; but what I most fear is that we should be recaptured by the Thorists. They will certainly search along the coast for us in the locality where they found us yesterday. They are not so stupid as not to guess that we will try to reach the Sofal.'

'If we can find the ocean, we might hide from them,' she suggested, 'until they had tired of the search and returned to Kapdor; then, if the Sofal is still there, we may yet be saved.'

'And if not, what?' I asked. 'Do you know anything about Noobol? Is there not some likelihood that we may find a friendly people somewhere in this land who will aid us to reach Vepaja again?'

She shook her head. 'I know little about Noobol,' she replied, 'but what little I have heard is not good. It is a sparsely settled land reaching, it is supposed, far into Strabol, the hot country, where no man may live. It is filled with wild beasts and savage tribes. There are scattered settlements along the coast, but most of these have been captured or reduced by the Thorists; the others, of course, would be equally dangerous, for they would consider all strangers as enemies.'

'The outlook is not bright,' I admitted, 'but we will not give up; we will find a way.'

'If any man can, I am sure that it is you,' she said.

Praise from Duare was sweet. In all the time that I had known her she had said only one other kind thing to me, and later she had retracted that.

'I could work miracles if only you loved me, Duare.'

She straightened haughtily. 'You will not speak of that,' she said coldly.

'Why do you hate me, Duare, who has given you only love?' I demanded.

'I do not hate you,' she replied, 'but you must not speak of love to the daughter of a jong. You should know that.

'We may be together for a long time, and you must remember that I may not listen to love from the lips of any man. Our very speaking together is a sin, but circumstances have made it impossible to do aught but sin in this respect.

'Before I was stolen from the house of the jong, no man had ever addressed me other than the members of my own family, except a few loyal and privileged members of my father's household; and until I should be twenty it were a sin in me and a crime in any man who should disregard this ancient law of the royal families of Amtor.'

'You forget,' I reminded her, 'that one man did address you in the house of your father.'

'An impudent knave,' she snapped, 'who should have died for his temerity.'

'Yet you did not inform on me.'

'Which made me equally guilty with you,' she replied, flushing. 'It is a shameful secret that will abide with me until my death,'

'A glorious memory that will always sustain my hope,' I told her.

'A false hope that you would do well to kill,' she said, and then, 'Why did you remind me of that day?' she demanded. 'When I think of it, I hate you; and I do not want to hate you.'

'That is something,' I suggested.

'Your affrontery and your hope feed on meager fare,'

'Which reminds me that it might be well for me to see if I can find something in the way of food for our bodies, too. They cannot subsist on so light a diet as hope.'

'There may be game in that forest,' she suggested, indicating the wood toward which we had been moving.

'We'll have a look,' I said, 'and then turn back and search for the illusive sea.'

A Venusan forest is a gorgeous sight. The foliage itself is rather pale – orchid, heliotrope, violet predominate – but the boles of the trees are gorgeous. They are of brilliant colours and often so glossy as to give the impression of having been lacquered.

The wood we were approaching was of the smaller varieties of trees, ranging in height from two hundred to three hundred feet and in diameter from twenty to thirty feet. There were none of the colossi of the island of Vepaja that reared their heads upward five thousand feet to penetrate the eternal inner cloud envelope of the planet.

The interior of the forest was illuminated by the mysterious Venusan ground glow, so that, unlike an earthly forest of similar magnitude upon a cloudy day, it was far from dark or gloomy. Yet there was something sinister about it. I cannot explain just what, nor why it should have been.

'I do not like this place,' said Duare, with a little shudder; 'there is no sight of animal, no sound of bird.'

'Perhaps we frightened them away,' I suggested.

'I do not think so; it is more likely that there is something else in the forest that has frightened them.'

I shrugged. 'Nevertheless, we must have food,' I reminded her, and I continued on into the forbidding, and at the same time gorgeous, wood that reminded me of a beautiful but wicked woman.

Several times I thought that I saw a suggestion of movement among the boles of distant trees, but when I reached them, there was nothing there. So I pressed on, deeper and deeper; and constantly a sense of impending evil grew stronger as I advanced. It was as though some terrible thing were lurking, ready to spring.

'There!' whispered Duare suddenly, pointing, 'There is something there, behind that tree. I saw it move.'

Something, just glimpsed from the corner of my eye, caught my attention to the left of us; and as I turned quickly in that direction something else dodged behind the bole of a large tree.

Duare wheeled about. 'There are things all around us!' she exclaimed.

'Can you make out what they are?' I asked.

'I thought that I saw a hairy hand, but I am not sure. They move quickly and keep always out of sight. Oh, let us go back! This is an evil place, and I am afraid,'

'Very well,' I agreed. 'Anyway, this doesn't seem to be a particularly good hunting ground; and after all that is all that we are looking for.'

As we turned to retrace our steps a chorus of hoarse shouts arose upon all sides of us – half human, half bestial, like the growls and roars of animals blending with the voices of men; and then, suddenly, from behind the boles of trees a score of hairy, manlike creatures sprang toward us.

Instantly I recognized them – kloonobargan – the same hairy, manlike creatures that had attacked the abductors of Duare, whom I had rescued from them. They were armed with crude bows and arrows and with slings from which they hurled rocks; but, as they closed upon us, it appeared that they wished to take us alive, as they launched no missiles at us.

But I had no mind to be thus taken so easily, nor to permit Duare to fall into the hands of these savage beast-men. Raising my pistol, I loosed the deadly r-ray upon them; and as some fell others leaped behind the boles of the trees.

'Do not let them take me,' said Duare in a level voice unshaken by emotion. 'When you see there is no further hope of escape, shoot me.'

The very thought of it turned me cold, but I knew that I should do it before permitting her to fall into the hands of these degraded creatures.

A nobargan showed himself, and I dropped him with my pistol; then they commenced to hurl rocks at me from behind. I wheeled and fired, and in the same instant my light went out.

When I regained consciousness, I was aware first of an incredible stench, and then of something rough rubbing against my skin, and of a rhythmic jouncing of my body. These sensations were vaguely appreciable in the first dim light of returning reason. With the return of full control of my faculties they were accounted for; I was being carried across the shoulder of a powerful nobargan.

The odor from his body was almost suffocating in its intensity, and the rough hair abrading my skin was only a trifle more annoying than the motion that his stride imparted to my body.

I sought to push myself from his shoulder; and, realizing that I was no longer unconscious, he dropped me to the ground. All about me were the hideous faces and hairy bodies of the kloonobargan and permeating the air the horrid stench that emanated from them.

They are, I am sure, the filthiest and most repulsive creatures that I have ever seen. Presumably, they are one of evolution's first steps from beast to man; but they are no improvement upon the beast. For the privilege of walking upright upon two feet, thus releasing their hands from the mean servitude of ages, and for the gift of speech they have sacrificed all that is fine and noble in the beast.

It is true, I believe, that man *descended* from the beasts; and it took him countless ages to rise to the level of his progenitors. In some respects he has not succeeded yet, even at the height of his vaunted civilization.

As I looked about, I saw Duare being dragged along by her hair by a huge nobargan. It was then that I discovered that my weapons had been taken from me. So low in the scale of intelligence are the kloonobargan that they cannot use the weapons of civilized man that fall into their hands, and so they had simply thrown mine aside.

But even though I was disarmed I could not see Duare suffering this ignominy and abuse without making an effort to aid her, and so I sprang forward before the beasts at my side could prevent and hurled myself upon the creature that dared to maltreat this daughter of a jong, this incomparable creature who had aroused within my breast the first exquisite tortures of love.

I seized him by one hairy arm and swung him around until he faced me, and then I struck him a terrific blow upon the chin that felled him. Instantly his fellows broke into loud laughter at his discomfiture; but that did not prevent them falling upon me and subduing me, and you may be assured that their methods were none too gentle.

As the brute that I had knocked down staggered to his

feet, his eyes fell upon me, and with a roar of rage he charged me. It might have fared badly with me had not another of them interfered. He was a burly creature, and when he interposed himself between me and my antagonist the latter paused.

'Stop!' commanded my ally, and had I heard a gorilla speak I could not have been more surprised. It was my introduction to a remarkable ethnological fact: all the races of mankind on Venus (at least those that I have come in contact with) speak the same tongue. Perhaps you can explain it; I cannot. When I have questioned Amtorian savants on the matter, they were merely dumfounded by the question; they could not conceive of any other condition; therefore there had never been any occasion to explain it.

Of course the languages differ in accordance with the culture of the nations; those with the fewest wants and the fewest experiences have the fewest words. The language of the kloonobargan is probably the most limited; a vocabulary of a hundred words may suffice them. But the basic root-words are the same everywhere.

The creature that had protected me, it presently developed, was the jong, or king, of this tribe; and I later learned that his act was not prompted by humanitarian considerations but by a desire to save me for another fate.

My act had not been entirely without good results, for during the balance of the march Duare was no longer dragged along by her hair. She thanked me for championing her; and that in itself was something worth being manhandled for, but she cautioned me against antagonizing them further.

Having discovered that at least one of these creatures could speak at least one word of the Amtorian language with which I was familiar, I sought to delve further in the hope that I might ascertain the purpose for which they had captured us.

'Why have you seized us?' I inquired of the brute that had spoken that single word, stop.

He looked at me in surprise, and those near enough to have overheard my question commenced to laugh and repeat it. Their laugh is far from light, airy, or reassuring. They bare their teeth in a grimace and emit a sound that is for all the world like the retching of *mal de mer*, and there is no laughter in their eyes. It took quite a stretch of my imagination to identify this as laughter.

'Albargan not know?' asked the jong. Albargan is, literally, no-hair-man, or without-hair-man, otherwise, hairless man.

'I do not know,' I replied. 'We were not harming you. We were searching for the sea coast where our people are.'

'Albargan find out soon,' and then he laughed again.

I tried to think of some way to bribe him into letting us go; but inasmuch as he had thrown away as useless the only things of value that we possessed, it seemed rather hopeless. I had nothing else to offer them.

'Tell me what you want most', I suggested, 'and perhaps I can get it for you if you will take us to the coast.'

'We have what we want,' he replied, and that answer made them all laugh.

I was walking close to Duare now, and she looked up at me with a hopeless expression. 'I am afraid we are in for it,' she said.

'It is all my fault. If I had had brains enough to find the ocean, this would never have happened.'

'Don't blame yourself. No one could have done more to protect and save me than have you. Please do not think that I do not appreciate it.'

That was a lot for Duare to say, and it was like a ray of sunshine in the gloom of my despondency. That is a simile entirely earthly, for there is no sunshine upon Venus. The relative proximity of the sun lights up the inner cloud envelope brilliantly, but it is a diffused light that casts no well-defined shadows nor produces contrasting highlights. There is an all-pervading glow from above that blends with the perpetual light emanations from the soil, and the resultant scene is that of a soft and beautiful pastel.

Our captors conducted us into the forest for a considerable distance; we marched practically all day. They spoke but seldom and then usually in monosyllables. They did not laugh again, and for that I was thankful. One can scarcely imagine a more disagreeable sound.

We had an opportunity to study them during this long march, and there is a question if either of us was quite sure in his own mind as to whether they were beast-like men or man-like beasts. Their bodies were entirely covered with hair; their feet were large and flat, and their toes were armed, like the fingers, with thick, heavy, pointed nails that resembled talons. They were large and heavy, with tremendous shoulders and necks. Their eyes were extremely close set in a baboon-like face; so that in some respects their heads bore a more striking similarity to the heads of dogs than of men. There was no remarkable dissimilarity between the males and the females, several of which were in the party; and the latter deported themselves the same as the bulls and appeared to be upon a plane of equality with these, carrying bows and arrows and slings for hurling rocks, a small supply of which they carried in skin pouches slung across their shoulders.

At last we reached an open space beside a small river where there stood a collection of the rudest and most primitive of shelters. These were constructed of branches of all sizes and shapes thrown together without symmetry and covered with a thatch of leaves and grasses. At the bottom of each was a single aperture through which one might crawl on hands and knees. They reminded me of the nests of pack rats built upon a Gargantuan scale.

Here were other members of the tribe, including several young; and at sight of us they rushed forward with excited cries. It was with difficulty that the jong and other members of the returning party kept them from tearing us to pieces.

The former hustled us into one of their evil-smelling nests and placed a guard before the entrance, more to protect us from his fellows, I suspect, than to prevent our escape.

The hut in which we were was filthy beyond words, but in the dim light of the interior I found a short stick with which I scraped aside the foul litter that covered the floor until I had uncovered a space large enough for us to lie down on the relatively clean earth.

We lay with our heads close to the entrance that we might get the benefit of whatever fresh air should find its way within. Beyond the entrance we could see a number of the savages digging two parallel trenches in the soft earth; each was about seven feet long and two feet wide.

'Why are they doing that? do you suppose,' asked Duare.

'I do not know,' I replied, although I had my suspicions; they looked remarkably like graves.

'Perhaps we can escape after they have gone to sleep tonight,' suggested Duare.

'We shall certainly take advantage of the first opportunity,' I replied, but there was no hope within me. I had a premonition that we should not be alive when the kloonobargan slept next.

'Look what they're doing now,' said Duare, presently; 'they're filling the trenches with wood and dry leaves. You don't suppose—?' she exclaimed, and caught her breath with a little gasp.

I placed a hand on one of hers and pressed it. 'We must not suppose anything,' I said. 'We must not conjure unnecessary horrors in our imaginations,' but I feared that she had guessed what I had already surmised – that my graves had become pits for cooking fires.

In silence we watched the creatures working about the two trenches. They built up walls of stone and earth about a foot high along each of the long sides of each pit; then they laid poles at intervals of a few inches across the tops of each pair of walls. Slowly before our eyes we saw two grills take shape.

'It is horrible,' whispered Duare.

Night came before the preparations were completed; then the savage jong came to our prison and commanded us to come forth. As we did so, we were seized by several shes and bulls who carried the long stems of tough jungle vines.

They threw us down and wound the vines about us. They were very clumsy and inept, not having sufficient intelligence to tie knots; but they accomplished their purpose in binding us by wrapping these fiber ropes around and around us until it seemed that it would be impossible to extricate ourselves even were we given the opportunity.

They bound me more securely than they did Duare, but even so the job was a clumsy one. Yet I guessed that it would be adequate to their purpose as they lifted us and laid us on the two parallel grills.

This done, they commenced to move slowly about us in a rude circle, while near us, and also inside the circle, squatted a bull that was engaged in the business of making fire in the most primitive manner, twirling the end of a sharpened stick in a tinder-filled hole in a log.

From the throats of the circling tribesmen issued strange sounds that were neither speech nor song, yet I guessed that they were groping blindly after song just as in their awkward circling they were seeking self-expression in the rhythm of the dance.

The gloomy wood, feebly illumined by the mysterious ground glow that is so distinctive a feature of Amtorian nights, brooded darkly above and about the weird and savage scene. In the distance the roar of a beast rumbled menacingly.

As the hairy men-things circled about us the bull beside the log at last achieved fire. A slow wisp of smoke rose lazily from the tinder. The bull added a few dry leaves and blew upon the feeble spark. A tiny flame burst forth, and a savage cry arose from the circling dancers. It was answered from the forest by the roar of the beast we had heard a short time before. Now it was closer, and was followed by the thundering voices of others of its kind.

The kloonobargan paused in their dancing to look apprehensively into the dark wood, voicing their displeasure in grumblings and low growls; then the bull beside the fire commenced to light torches, a quantity of which lay prepared beside him; and as he passed them out the others resumed their dancing.

The circle contracted, and occasionally a dancer would leap in and pretend to light the faggots beneath us. The blazing torches illumined the weird scene, casting grotesque shadows that leaped and played like gigantic demons.

The truth of our predicament was now all too obvious, though I know that we had both suspected it since long before we had been laid upon the grills – we were to be barbecued to furnish the flesh for a cannibal feast. The very horror of it fascinated me.

Duare turned her head toward me. 'Goodbye, Carson Napier!' she whispered. 'Before I go, I want you to know that I appreciate the sacrifice you have made for me. But for me you would be aboard the Sofal now, safe among loyal friends."

'I would rather be here with you, Duare,' I replied, 'than to be anywhere else in the universe without you.'

She turned her face from me and did not reply, and then a huge, shaggy bull leaped in with a flaming torch and ignited the faggots at the lower end of the trench beneath her.

CHAPTER 4

FIRE

FROM the surrounding forest came the roars of hungry beasts; but the sounds affected me none, so horrified was I by the hideous fate that had overtaken Duare.

I saw her struggling with her bonds, as I struggled with mine; but in the clumsily wound coils of the tough lianas we were helpless. Little flames below her feet were licking the larger faggots. Duare had managed to wriggle toward the head of the grill, so that the flames were not as yet directly beneath her; and she was still struggling with her bonds.

I had been paying little attention to the kloonobargan, but suddenly I realized that they had ceased their crude dancing and singing. Glancing toward them, I saw that they were standing looking off into the forest, the torches dangling in their hands, nor had they as yet lighted the faggots beneath me.

Now I took note again of the thunderous roars of the beasts; they sounded very close. I saw dim figures slinking amidst the shadows of the trees and blazing eyes gleaming in the half light.

Presently a huge beast slunk out of the forest into the clearing, and I recognized it from the description that Sov had given Moosko. I saw the stiff hair-like bristles. It was standing erect along the shoulders, neck, and spine. I saw the white, longitudinal stripes marking the reddish coat, and the bluish belly and the great, snarling jaws. The creature was a tharban, a huge lion-like carnivore.

The kloonobargan were watching it also. Presently they commenced to cry out against it and cast rocks at it from their slings, in an obvious effort to frighten it away; but it did not retreat. Instead, it came slowly closer, roaring horribly; and behind it came others - two, three a dozen, two score - slinking from the concealing shadows of the forest. All were roaring, and the hideous volume of those mighty voices shook the ground.

And now the kloonobargan fell back. The great beasts

invading the village increased their speed, and suddenly the hairy savages turned and fled. After them, roaring and growling, sprang the tharbans (I am abandoning the Amtorian plural prefix, kloo, in favor of the less cumbersome and more familiar English form).

The speed of the clumsy-appearing nobargans was a revelation to me, and as they disappeared into the dark mazes of the forest it was not apparent that the tharbans were gaining on them, though as the latter raced past me they seemed to be moving as swiftly as a charging lion.

The beasts paid no attention to Duare or me. I doubt that they even saw us, their whole attention being fixed upon the fleeing savages.

Now I turned again toward Duare just in time to see her roll herself from the grill to the ground as the licking flames were about to reach her feet. For the moment she was safe, and I breathed a little prayer of thanksgiving. But what of the future? Must we lie here until inevitably the nobargans returned or some prowling beast of the forest discovered us?

Duare looked up at me. She was struggling steadily with her bonds. 'I believe that I can free myself,' she said; 'I am not bound so tightly as you. If only I can do it before they return!'

I watched her in silence. After what seemed an eternity, she got one arm free. After that the rest was comparatively easy, and when she was free, she quickly released me.

Like two phantoms, in the eerie light of the Amtorian night we faded into the shadows of the mysterious forest; and you may rest assured that we took a direction opposite to that in which the lions and the cannibals had disappeared.

The momentary elation that escape from the clutches of the nobargans had given me passed quickly as I considered our situation. We two were alone, unarmed, and lost in a strange country that brief experience had already demonstrated to be filled with dangers and that imagination peopled with a hundred menaces even more frightful than those we had encountered.

Raised in the carefully guarded seclusion of the house of a jong, Duare was quite as ignorant of the flora, the fauna, and the conditions existing in the land of Noobol as was I, an inhabitant of a far distant planet; and notwithstanding our culture, our natural intelligence, and my considerable physical strength we were still little better than babes in the woods.

We had been walking in silence, listening and looking for some new menace to our recently won respite from death, when Duare spoke in low tones, as one might who is addressing a question to himself.

'And should I ever return to the house of my father, the jong, who will believe the story that I shall tell? Who will believe that I, Duare, the daughter of the jong, passed through such incredible dangers alive?' She turned and looked up into my face. 'Do you believe, Carson Napier, that I ever shall return to Vepaja?'

'I do not know, Duare,' I replied honestly. 'To be perfectly frank, it seems rather hopeless inasmuch as neither of us knows where we are or where Vepaja is, or what further dangers confront us in this barbaric land.

'And what if we never find Vepaja, Duare? What if you and I go on for many years together? Must it always be as strangers, as enemies? Is there no hope for me, Duare? No hope to win your love?'

'Have I not told you that you must not speak to me of love? It is wicked for a girl under twenty to speak or even think of love; and for me, the daughter of a jong, it is even worse. If you persist, I will not talk to you at all.'

After this we walked on in silence for a long time. We were both very tired and hungry and thirsty, but for the time we subordinated all other desires to that of escaping the clutches of the nobargans; but at last I realized that Duare had about reached the limit of her endurance, and I called a halt.

Selecting a tree, the lower branches of which were within easy reach, we climbed upward until I chanced upon a rude nest-like platform that might have been built by some arboreal creature or formed by debris falling from above during a storm. It lay upon two almost horizontal branches that extended from the bole of the tree in about the same plane, and was amply large enough to accommodate both of us.

As we stretched our tired bodies upon this mean yet none the less welcome couch, the growl of some great beast arose from the ground beneath to assure us that we had found sanctuary none to soon. What other dangers menaced us from arboreal creatures, I did not know; but any thought of keeping wakeful vigil was dissipated by the utter exhaustion of both my mind and my body. I doubt that I could have kept awake much longer even in the act of walking.

As I was dozing off, I heard Duare's voice. It sounded sleepy and far away. 'Tell me, Carson Napier,' she said; 'what is this thing called love?'

*

When I awoke, another day had come. I looked up at the mass of foliage lying motionless in the air above me, and for a moment I had difficulty in recalling my surroundings and the events that had led me to this place. I turned my head and saw Duare lying beside me, and then it all came back to me. I smiled a little as I recalled that last, sleepy question she had asked me – a question that I realized now I had not answered. I must have fallen asleep as it was propounded.

For two days we moved steadily in what we thought was the direction of the ocean. We subsisted on eggs and fruit, which we found in abundance. There was a great deal of life in the forest – strange birds such as no earthly eye had ever gazed upon before, monkey-like creatures that raced, chattering, through the trees, reptiles, herbivorous and carnivorous animals. Many of the latter were large and predacious. The worst of these, that we encountered, were the tharbans; but their habit of senseless roaring and growling preserved us from them by warning us of their proximity.

Another creature that caused us some bad moments was the basto. I had met this animal once before, that time that Kamlot and I had gone out upon our disastrous tarel gathering excursion; and so I was prepared to take to the trees with Duare the instant that we sighted one of these beasts.

Above the eyes, the head of a basto resembles the American bison, having the same short powerful horns and the thick, curly hair upon its poll and forehead. Its eyes are small and red rimmed. The hide is blue and about the same texture as that of an elephant, with sparsely growing hairs except upon the head and tip of the tail, where the hair is thicker and longer. The beast stands very high at the shoulders but slopes downward rapidly to the rump. It has a tremendous depth of shoulder and exceedingly short, stocky forelegs, which are supplied with three-toed feet. Its hind legs are longer, more slender, and the hind feet are smaller. The forelegs carry fully three-quarters of the beast's weight. The muzzle is similar to that of a boar, except that it is broader, and carries two heavy, curved tusks.

The basto is an ill-tempered. omnivorous brute, always looking for trouble, that it is well to avoid. Between him and the tharban Duare and I became most proficient tree climbers during the first few days that we wandered through the forest.

My two greatest handicaps in this encounter with the utmost primitive were lack of weapons and my inability to make fire. The latter was probably the worse, since, without a knife, fire was indispensable to the fashioning of weapons.

At every rest I experimented. Duare became inoculated with the virus of the quest, and fire became our sole aim. We talked about little else and were forever experimenting with different combinations of wood and with bits of rock that we picked up along the way.

All my life I had read of primitive men making fire in various ways, and I tried them all. I blistered my hands twirling fire sticks. I knocked bits of flesh off my fingers striking pieces of stone together. At last I was on the point of giving up in disgust.

'I don't believe anyone ever made fire,' I grumbled.

'You saw the nobargan make it,' Duare reminded me.

'There's a catch in it somewhere,' I insisted.

'Are you going to give up?' she asked.

'Of course not. It's like golf. Most people never learn to play it, but very few give up trying. I shall probably continue my search for fire until death overtakes me, or Prometheus descends to Venus as he did to earth.'

'What is golf and who is Prometheus?' demanded Duare.

'Golf is a mental disorder and Prometheus a fable.'

'I don't see how they can help you very much.'

I was squatting over a little pile of tinder laboriously knocking together various bits of rock that we had collected during the day.

'Neither do I,' I replied, viciously striking two new

specimens together. A string of sparks shot from the two rocks and ignited the tinder! 'I apologize to Prometheus,' I cried; 'he is no fable.'

With the aid of this fire I was able to fashion a bow and to make and sharpen a spear and arrows. I strung the bow with a fiber from a tough liana, and I feathered my arrows gaily with the plumage of birds.

Duare was much interested in this work. She gathered feathers, split them, and bound them to the arrows with the long blades of a very tough grass that grew in profusion throughout the forest. Our work was facilitated by the use of bits of stone we had found so shaped that they made excellent scrapers.

I cannot express the change that came over me with the possession of weapons. I had come to feel like a hunted beast whose only defense is flight, and that is a most unhappy situation for the man who wishes to impress the object of his love with his heroic qualities.

I really cannot say that I had any such intention in my mind at any time, yet with the growing realization of my futility and the consequent development of an inferiority complex, I really did come to wish that I might cut a better figure before Duare.

Now I stepped out with a new stride. I was the hunter rather than the hunted. My pitiful, inadequate little weapons swept all doubts from my mind. I was now equal to any emergency.

'Duare,' I exclaimed, 'I am going to find Vepaja; I am going to take you home!'

She looked at me questioningly. 'The last time we spoke of that,' she reminded me, 'you said that you hadn't the remotest idea where Vepaja was and that if you had, you couldn't hope to get there.'

'That,' I said, 'was several days ago. Things are different now. Now, Duare, we are going hunting; we are going to have meat for dinner. You walk behind me so as not to frighten the game."

I moved forward with my old assurance and, perhaps, a little incautiously. Duare followed a few paces in the rear. There was considerable undergrowth in this portion of the forest, more than I had encountered before, and I could not see very far in any direction. We were following what appeared to be a game trail, along which I advanced boldly but silently.

Presently I saw a movement in the foliage ahead and then what appeared to be the outlines of some large animal. Almost instantly the silence of the forest was broken by the thunderous bellow of a basto, and there was a great crashing in the undergrowth.

'Take to the trees, Duare!' I cried, and at the same time I turned and ran back to assist her in climbing out of danger; and then Duare stumbled and fell.

Again the basto bellowed, and a quick backward glance revealed the mighty creature in the trail only a few paces in my rear. He was not charging; but he was advancing, and I could see that he would be upon us before we could possibly climb to safety, because of the slight delay occasioned by Duare's fall.

There appeared to be but one course of action open to me – I must delay the beast until Duare had gained a place of safety. I recalled how Kamlot had slain one of the creatures by distracting its attention from himself to a leafy branch held in his left hand and then plunged his keen sword behind the shoulder down into the heart. But I had no leafy branch and only a crude wooden spear.

He was almost upon me, his red rimmed eyes blazing, his white tusks gleaming. He loomed as large as an elephant to my excited imagination. He put his head down, another thunderous roar rumbled from his cavernous chest; and then he charged.

CHAPTER 5

THE BULL AND THE LION

AS THE basto bore down upon me, my only thought was to divert his attention from Duare until she should be safely out of his reach. It all happened so quickly that I imagine I had no time to think of my own almost certain fate.

The brute was so close to me when he started his charge that he attained no great speed. He came straight toward me with his head lowered, and so mighty and awe inspiring was he that I did not even consider attempting to stop him with my puny and futile weapons.

Instead, I threw them to the ground, all my thoughts centered upon one objective – to save myself from being impaled upon those short, powerful horns.

I grasped them, one with each hand, as the basto struck me; and, thanks to my unusual strength, I succeeded in breaking the force of the impact as well as diverting the horns from my vitals.

The instant that he felt my weight, the brute ripped upward with his head in an effort to gore and toss me, and in the latter he succeeded beyond anything that I might have expected and, I imagine, beyond what he intended.

With almost the force of an explosion I was hurtled upward to crash through the foliage and the branches of the tree above. Fortunately my head came in contact with no large limb, and so I retained consciousness through it all. Very happily for me, I also retained my presence of mind; and, clutching frantically, I succeeded in grasping a branch across which my body had half fallen. From there I dragged myself to the safety of a larger limb.

My first thought was of Duare. Was she safe? Had she been able to climb out of danger before the basto disposed of me and was upon her, or had he reached and gored her?

My fears were almost immediately allayed by the sound of her voice. "Oh, Carson, Carson! Are you hurt?' she cried. The anguish of her tones was ample reward for any hurts I might have sustained.

'I think not,' I replied; 'just shaken up a bit. Are you all right? Where are you?'

'Here, in the next tree. Oh, I thought he had killed you!'

I was testing out my joints and feeling of myself for possible injuries; but I discovered nothing more serious than bruises, and of these I had plenty.

As I was examining myself, Duare made her way along interlocking branches; and presently she was at my side. 'You're bleeding,' she exclaimed. 'You *are* hurt.'

'These are nothing but scratches,' I assured her; 'only my pride is hurt.'

'Your pride! Why should that be hurt?'

'I was so sure of myself just a moment ago, so self-satisfied with my new and wonderful weapons; and now look at me! disarmed and glad to be up a tree and safe from the first creature I met.'

'You have nothing to be ashamed of; you should be very proud of what you did. I saw. I glanced behind me as I got to my feet, and I saw you standing right in the path of that terrible beast so that it would not reach me.'

'Perhaps,' I suggested, 'I was too terrified to run – just paralyzed by fear.'

She smiled and shook her head. 'I know better than that; I know you too well.'

'Any risk would be worth taking if it won your approval.'

She was silent for a moment, looking down at the basto. The brute was pawing the ground and bellowing. Occasionally it would pause and look up at us.

'It seems very angry,' said Duare. 'I wish it would go away.'

'It is waiting for us to fall out of the tree, I should judge by the way it keeps looking up at us. I wonder how much longer it will hang around.'

'We could get away from it by going through the trees,' suggested Duare. 'They grow very close together here.'

'And abandon my new weapons?' I demanded.

'Oh, I forgot them. Of course we mustn't do that.'

'He'll probably go away in a few minutes,' I prophesied, 'as soon as he realizes that we are not coming down.'

But he didn't go away in a few minutes. He bellowed and

pawed and gored the ground for half an hour, and then he lay down beneath the tree.

'That fellow's an optimist,' I remarked.

'Why? What makes you think that?'

'He thinks that if he waits long enough we'll probably come down of our own volition,' I explained.

Duare laughed. 'Maybe he thinks we'll die of old age and fall down.'

'That's a joke on him; he doesn't know that we have been inoculated with the serum of longevity.'

'In the meantime, the joke is on us; and I am getting hungry.'

'Look, Duare!' I whispered, as I caught sight of something dimly visible through the tangled undergrowth beyond the basto.

'What is it?' she asked.

'I don't know, but it's something large,'

'It is creeping silently through the brush, Carson. Do you suppose it is something that has caught our scent, some other terrible beast of prey?'

'Well, we are up a tree,' I reassured her.

'Yes, and many of these creatures climb trees. I wish you had your weapons.'

'If that basto would look the other way for a minute, I'd go down and get them.'

'No, you mustn't do that – one or the other of them would get you.'

'Here it comes now, Duare! Look!'

'It's a tharban,' she whispered.

The evil face of the fierce carnivore was protruding from the underbrush a short distance beyond and behind the basto. The latter did not see it, nor did his nostrils catch the scent of the great cat-like creature.

'It's not looking at us,' I said; 'it's watching the basto.'

'Do you suppose –' commenced Duare, and then her words were drowned by the most blood-curdling scream I have ever heard.

It came from the savage throat of the tharban at the instant that it sprang toward the basto. The latter beast, lumbering to its feet, was caught at a disadvantage. The tharban leaped full upon its back, sinking talons and fangs deep into the tough flesh.

The bellowing of the basto mingled with the roars and growls of the tharban in a hideous diapason of bestial rage that seemed to rock the forest.

The huge bull wheeled in a frenzy of pain and sought to sink its horn in the thing upon its back. The tharban struck viciously at the savage face, raking downward from poll to muzzle, tearing hide and flesh to the bone, one great talon ripping an eye from its socket.

Its head a bloody mass of torn flesh, the basto threw itself upon its back with almost cat-like agility; seeking to crush the life from its tormentor; but the tharban leaped to one side and, as the bull scrambled to its feet, sprang in again.

This time the basto, wheeling with lowered head and incredible swiftness, caught the tharban full upon its horns and tossed it high into the foliage of the tree above.

A screaming, clawing hellion of unrestrained primitive rage and hate. the great carnivore hurtled upward within a few feet of Duare and me; and then, still clawing and screaming, it fell back.

Like a huge cat, that it most closely resembled, it came down feet first. With ready horns and tail stiffly erect, the basto waited to catch it and toss it again. Full on those powerful horns the tharban fell; but when the basto surged upward with all the strength of that mighty, bulging neck, the tharban did not soar upward into the tree again. With powerful claws and mighty jaws it clung to the head and neck of its antagonist. It raked shoulder and throat as the basto attempted to shake it loose. With fearful strokes of its talons it was tearing the basto to shreds.

In a bloody welter of gore, the stricken creature, now totally blinded by the loss of its remaining eye, wheeled in a grotesque and futile pirouette of death; but still its screaming Nemesis clung to it, tearing, striking in mad, blind rage, its hideous cries mingling with the now shrill death bellowings of the stricken bull.

Suddenly the basto stopped in its tracks, its feet spread wide apart. For a moment it stood there swaying weakly. Blood was gushing from its neck in such a torrent that I was positive its jugular must have been severed; I knew that the end must be near and only wondered at the unbelievable tenacity with which the creature clung to life.

Nor was the tharban in an enviable state. Once badly gored and now impaled upon those two mighty horns, the blood of his terrible wounds mingling with the blood of his intended victim, his chances of survival were as negligible as those of the weaving bull, already seemingly dead upon his feet.

But how could I guess the inconceivable vitality of these mighty creatures!

With a sudden shake of his horns the bull stiffened; then he lowered his head and charged blindly, apparently with all the strength and vigor of unimpaired vitality.

It was to be a short charge. With terrific impact he struck the bole of the tree in which we were crouching. The branch upon which we sat swayed and snapped like a loose spar in a gale, and Duare and I were toppled from our perch.

Clutching futilely for support, we shot downward on top of the tharban and the basto. For an instant I was terrified for Duare's safety, but there was no need for apprehension. Neither of these mighty engines of destruction turned upon us; neither moved. Except for a few convulsive shudders they lay still in death. And thus Death saved us from death.

The tharban had been caught between the bole of the tree and the massive poll of the basto and crushed to pulp; the basto had died as it wreaked its final, fearful vengeance on the tharban.

Duare and I had rolled to the ground beside the bodies of these mighty Titans; and now, uninjured, we sprang to our feet. Duare was pale and a trifle shaken, but she smiled bravely up into my face.

'Our hunting was more successful than we dreamed,' she said; 'here is meat enough for many men.'

'Kamlot told me that there was nothing like a basto steak grilled over a wood fire.'

'They are delicious. My mouth is watering already.'

'And mine, too, Duare; but without a knife we are still a long way from the steak. Look at that thick hide.'

Duare looked crestfallen. 'Did ever two people have such continuous bad luck!' she exclaimed. 'But never mind,' she added. 'Get your weapons, and perhaps we shall find something small enough to tear to pieces or cook whole.'

'Wait!' I exclaimed, opening the pocket pouch that hung

over my shoulder by a stout cord. 'I have a piece of stone with a sharp edge that I used for scraping my bow and arrows. I may be able to hack out a meal with it.'

It was a laborious job; but I finally succeeded, and while I was engaged upon this crude and ragged butchery Duare gathered tinder and wood and surprised us both by starting a fire. She was very happy and excited over her success, and proud, too. In all her pampered life at home she had never been required to do a practical thing, and the reward of even this small accomplishment filled her with joy.

That meal was a memorable one; it was epochal. It marked the emergence of primitive man from the lower orders of life. He had achieved fire; he had fashioned weapons; he had made his kill (figuratively, in this case); and now for the first time he was eating cooked food. And I liked to carry the metaphor a little further in this instance and think of the partner of his achievements as his mate. I sighed as I thought of the happiness that might be ours did Duare but return my love.

'What's the matter?' demanded Duare. 'Why do you sigh?'

'I am sighing because I am not really a primitive man instead of a poor, weak imitation of one.'

'Why do you want to be a primitive man?' she inquired.

'Because primitive man was not bound by silly conventions,' I replied. 'If he wanted a woman and she did not want him, he grabbed her by the hair and dragged her to his lair; it was all very simple.'

'I am glad that I did not live in those times,' said Duare. 'I would not like to be dragged around by the hair. If any man tried to drag me by the hair, I would kill him.'

*

For several days we wandered on through the forest. I knew that we were hopelessly lost, but I was anxious to get out of that gloomy wood. It was getting on our nerves. I managed to kill small game with my spear and my arrows; there was an abundance of fruit and nuts, and water was plentiful. In the matter of food we lived like kings, and we were fortunate in our encounters with the more formidable creatures that we met. Fortunately for us we saw none that was arboreal, though I am positive that this was merely by the luckiest chance, for the woods of Amtor harbor many terrible creatures that live wholly in the trees.

Duare, notwithstanding all the hardships and dangers she was constantly undergoing, seldom complained. She remained remarkably cheerful in the face of what was now palpably the absolute certainty that we could never hope to find the distant island where her father was king. Sometimes she was sober and silent for long periods, and I guessed that at these times she was sorrowing; but she did not share her sorrows with me. I wished that she would; we often share our sorrows with those we love.

But one day she suddenly sat down and commenced to cry. I was so surprised that I just stood there for several minutes staring at her before I could think of anything to say, and then I didn't think of anything very brilliant.

'Why, Duare!' I cried. 'What's the matter? Are you ill?'

She shook her head and sought to stifle her sobs. 'I'm sorry,' she managed to say at last. 'I didn't mean to; I've tried not to; but this forest! Oh, Carson, it's on my nerves; it haunts me even in my sleep. It is endless; it goes on and on forever – gloomy, forbidding, filled with terrible dangers. There!' she exclaimed, and rising she shook her head as though to dispel unwelcome visions. 'I'm all right now; I won't do it again.' She smiled through her tears.

I wanted to take her in my arms and comfort her – oh, how badly I wanted to! But I only laid a hand upon her shoulder. 'I know just how you feel,' I told her. 'I've felt the same way for days. I'm only sorry that I can't cry too; it would be a relief. I have to take it out by swearing to myself.

'But it can't last forever, Duare. There must be an end to it pretty soon; and, anyway, you must remember that the forest has fed us and sheltered us and protected us.'

'As a jailer feeds and shelters and protects the criminal condemned to die,' she responded dully. 'Come! let's not speak of it any more.'

Once again the underbrush was thick, and we were following a game trail that was as erratic as most game trails. I think it was this thick brush that depressed Duare even more than the forest itself. I know it always depresses me. The trail was wide and we were walking abreast when suddenly at a turning the forest seemed to disappear in front of us before our eyes. There was a void staring us in the face, and beyond that, far, far away, the outlines of distant mountains.

CHAPTER 6

Down the Escarpment

Wonderingly we advanced until we stood upon the brink of a lofty escarpment. Far below, at least five thousand feet, a great valley spread before our eyes. Far, far away, across it, we saw the outlines of the distant mountains that hemmed it upon that side; but to the right and left its extent was shrouded in the mists of distance.

During the days that we had been wandering in the forest we must have been climbing steadily, but the ascent had been so gradual that we had scarcely noticed it. Now, the effect of coming suddenly upon this mighty depression was startling. It was as though I were looking into a deep pit that lay far below sea level. This impression, however, was soon dispelled, for in the distance I saw a great river winding along the bed of the valley; and I knew that it must run downward to some sea.

'A new world!' breathed Duare. 'How beautiful by contrast with this frightful forest!'

'Let us hope that it will be no less kind to us than the forest has been.'

'How could it be otherwise than kind? It is so beautiful,' she replied. 'There must be people living there, generous, kindly people as lovely as their lovely valley. There could be no evil where there is so much beauty. Perhaps they will help us to return to Vepaja. I am sure they will.'

'I hope so, Duare,' I said.

'See!' she exclaimed. 'There are little rivers running into the big river, and there are level plains dotted with trees, and there are forests, too, but no terrible forest that stretches on and on seemingly without end as this that we are escaping.

'Do you see any cities or signs of man, Carson?'

I shook my head. 'I cannot be positive. We are very high above the valley; and the large river, where it is probable the cities would be, is far away. Only a very great city with tall buildings would be visible from here, and the haze that hangs over the valley might even hide a large city from us. We shall have to go down into the valley to find out.'

'I can scarcely wait,' exclaimed Duare.

The trail on which we had approached the edge of the escarpment turned sharply to the left and skirted the brink, but from it a smaller trail branched and dropped over the edge.

This trail was little better than a faintly marked foot path, and it zigzagged down the almost vertical face of the escarpment in a manner calculated to send the cold chills up one's back if he happened to be affected by such things.

'Few creatures go up and down here,' remarked Duare, as she looked over the edge of the escarpment at the dizzy trail.

'Perhaps we had better go on farther; there may be an easier way down,' I suggested, thinking that she might be fearful.

'No,' she demurred, 'I wanted to get out of the forest, and here is my chance. Something has gone up and down here; and if something else has, we can.'

'Take my hand, then; it is very steep.'

She did as I bid, and I also handed her my spear to use as a staff. Thus we started the perilous descent. Even now I hate to recall it. It was not only fraught with danger but it was exceedingly exhausting. A dozen times I thought that we were doomed; seemingly it was impossible to descend farther, and certainly it would have been impossible to retrace our steps to the summit, for there had been places where we had lowered ourselves over ledges that we could not have again scaled.

Duare was very brave. She amazed me. Not only was her courage remarkable, but her endurance was almost unbelievable in one so delicately moulded. And she kept cheerful and good-natured. Often she laughed when she would slip and almost fall, when a fall would have meant certain death.

'I said,' she recalled, once while we were resting, 'that something must have come up and down this trail. Now I wonder what manner of creature it may be.'

'Perhaps it is a mountain goat,' I suggested. 'I can think of nothing else that might do it.'

She did not know what a mountain goat was, and I knew

of no Venusan animal with which to compare it. She thought that a mistal might easily go up and down such a trail. I had never heard of this animal, but from her description I judged it to be a rat-like animal about the size of a house cat.

As we were starting down again after a rest, I heard a noise below us and looked over the edge of the ledge on which we stood to see what had caused it.

'We are about to have our curiosity satisfied,' I whispered to Duare. 'Here comes the trail maker.'

'Is it a mistal?' she asked.

'No, nor a mountain goat; but it is just the sort of a creature that might most easily cling to this vertical pathway. I don't know what you Amortians call it. Take a look; perhaps you will recognize it.'

It was a huge, hideous lizard about twenty feet in length that was climbing sluggishly upward toward our position.

Leaning on my shoulder, Duare glanced downward over the ledge. She voiced a low gasp of terror. 'I think it is a vere,' she said, 'and if it is, we are in for it. I have never seen one, but I have read of them in books and seen their pictures; this one looks like the pictures I have seen.'

'Are they dangerous?' I asked.

'They are deadly,' she replied. 'We wouldn't have a chance against a vere.'

'See if you can climb back out of the way,' I said to Duare. 'I will try to hold it here until you are safe;' then I turned toward the creature crawling slowly upward. It was covered with scales of red, black, and yellow arranged in intricate designs. Its coloration and ornamentation were beautiful, but right there its beauty stopped. It had a head not unlike that of a crocodile, and along each side of its upper jaw was a row of gleaming white horns. Across the top and down the sides of its head sprawled a single huge eye of myriad facets.

It had not discovered us yet, but in another half minute it would be upon us. I loosened a bit of rock near my hand and hurled it down, thinking I might turn the creature back. The missile struck it on the snout, and with a grunt it raised its head and saw me.

Its great jaws opened, and out shot the most prodigious

tongue I had ever seen. Like lightning it curled about me and snapped me toward those gaping jaws from which was issuing a harsh, screaming whistle.

All that saved me from being instantly engulfed was the fact that I was a little too large a mouthful for the creature to negotiate with ease. I wedged crosswise of his snout, and there I fought with all my strength to keep from being dragged into that rapacious maw.

It was a great slimy, toothless, sucking gullet that I struggled to escape. Evidently the creature swallowed its prey whole, its horns being probably solely for defense. From that repulsive throat issued a fetid odor that almost overpowered me. I think that it may have been a poisonous exhalation that was intended to anaesthetize its victims. I felt myself growing weak and dizzy, and then I saw Duare at my side.

She was grasping my spear in both hands and lunging viciously at the horrid face of the vere. How small and frail and inadequate she looked to be pitting herself against this fearsome creature! and how magnificent!

She was risking her life to save mine, and yet she did not love me. Still, it was not incredible – there are noble qualities far more unselfish than love. Loyalty is of these. But I could not permit her to sacrifice her life for loyalty.

'Run, Duare!' I cried. 'You can't save me – I am done for. Run while you can, or it will kill us both.'

She paid no attention to me, but thrust again. This time the spear tore into the many faceted eye. With a shrill whistle of pain, the reptile turned upon Duare and sought to strike her with its gleaming horns; but she stood her ground and, thrusting again, drove the weapon between the distended jaws, drove it deep and far into the pink flesh of that repulsive maw.

The spear point must have pierced the tongue, for it suddenly went limp; and I rolled from its encircling grasp to the ground.

Instantly I was on my feet again and, seizing Duare's arm, dragged her to one side as the vere charged blindly. It brushed past us, whistling and screaming, and then turned, but in the wrong direction.

It was then that I realized that the creature had been totally blinded by the wound in its eye. Taking a perilous risk, I threw an arm about Duare and slid over the edge of the ledge upon which the brute had encountered us, for to have remained even an instant where we were would have meant being maimed or hurled to our doom by the viciously lashing tail of the frenzied lizard.

Fortune favored us, and we came safely to rest upon another ledge at a slightly lower level. Above us we could hear the whistling scream of the vere and the thudding of his tail against the rocky escarpment.

Fearing that the creature might descend upon us, we hurried on, taking even great risks than we had before; nor did we stop until we had reached comparatively level ground near the foot of theescarpment. Then we sat down to rest. We were both panting from our exertions.

'You were wonderful!' I said to Duare. 'You risked your life to save mine. You must care a little.'

'Perhaps I was just afraid to be left alone.' she said. 'I may have been entirely selfish,'

'I don't believe that,' I remonstrated. The truth was that I didn't want to believe it. Another implication was far sweeter to my ego.

'Anyhow,' remarked Duare, 'we found out what made the trail up the escarpment.'

'And that our beautiful valley may not be as secure as it looks,' I added.

'But the creature was going out of the valley up into the forest,' she argued; 'that is probably where it lived.'

'However, we had best be on our guard constantly.'

'And now you have no spear; and that is a real loss, for it is because of the spear that you are alive.'

'Down there a little way,' I indicated, pointing, 'is a winding strip of wood that seems to be following the meanderings of a stream. There we can find material for another spear and also water – I am as dry as a bone.'

'So am I,' said Duare, 'and hungry too. Perhaps you can kill another basto.'

I laughed. 'This time I shall make you a spear and a bow and arrows, too. From what you have already done, you seem to be better able to kill bastos than I.'

Leisurely we walked toward the wood, which was about a mile away, through soft grass of a pale violet hue. Flowers grew in profusion on every hand. There were purple flowers and blue flowers and pale yellow flowers; and their foliage, like them, was strange and unearthly. There were flowers and leaves of colors that have no name, colors such as no earthly eye ever had seen before.

Such things bear in upon me the strange isolation of our senses. Each sense lives in a world of its own, and though it lives a lifetime with its fellow senses, it knows nothing of their worlds.

My eyes see a color; but my fingers, my ears, my nose, my palate may never know that color. I cannot even describe it so that any of your senses may perceive it as I perceive it, if it is a new color that you have never seen. Even less well might I describe an odor or a flavor or the feel of some strange substance. Only by comparison might I make you see the landscape that stretched before our eyes, and there is nothing in your world with which I may compare it – the glowing fog bank overhead, the pale, soft pastels of field and forest and distant misty mountains – no dense shadows and no high lights – strange and beautiful and weird – intriguing, provocative, compelling, always beckoning one on to further investigation, to new adventure.

All about us the plain between the escarpment and the forest was dotted with trees; and, lying beneath them or grazing in the open, were animals that were entirely new to my experience either here or on Earth. That several distinct families and numerous genera were represented was apparent to even a cursory survey.

Some were large and cumbersome, others were small and dainty. All were too far away for me to note them in detail; and for that I was glad, for I guessed that among that array of wild beasts there must be some at least which might prove dangerous to man. But, like all animals except hungry carnivores and men, they showed no disposition to attack us so long as we did not interfere with them or approach them too closely.

'I see that we shall not go hungry here,' remarked Duare.

'I hope some of those little fellows are good to eat,' I laughed.

'I am sure that big one under the tree is delicious; the one looking at us,' and she pointed to an enormous, shaggy creature as large as an elephant. Duare had a sense of humor.

'Possibly it entertains the same idea concerning us,' I suggested; 'here it comes!'

The huge beast was walking toward us. The forest was still a hundred yards away.

'Shall we run?' asked Duare.

'I am afraid that would be fatal. You know, it is almost instinctive for a beast to pursue any creature that runs away from it. I think the best course for us to follow is to continue steadily towards the forest without seeming haste. If the thing does not increase its speed, we shall reach the trees ahead of it; if we run for it, the chances are that it will overtake us, for of all created things man seems to be about the slowest.'

As we proceeded, we constantly cast backward glances at the shaggy menace trailing us. He lumbered along, exhibiting no signs of excitement; but his long strides were eating up the distance between us. I saw that he would overtake us before we reached the forest. I felt utterly helpless, with my puny bow and my tiny arrows, before this towering mountain of muscle.

'Quicken your pace a little, Duare,' I directed.

She did as I bid, but after a few steps she glanced back.

'Why don't you come, too?' she demanded.

'Don't argue,' I snapped a little shortly. 'Do as I bid you.'

She stopped and waited for me. 'I shall do as I please,' she informed me, 'and it does not please me to let you make this sacrifice for me. If you are to be killed, I shall be killed with you. Furthermore, Carson Napier, please remember that I am the daughter of a jong and am not accustomed to being ordered about.'

'If there were not more pressing matters to occupy me I would spank you,' I growled.

She looked at me, horrified; then she stamped one little foot in rage and commenced to cry. 'You take advantage of me because there is no one to protect me,' she spluttered. 'I hate you, you — you —— '

'But I am trying to protect you, Duare; and you are only making it harder for me.'

'I don't want any of your protection; I would rather be dead. It is more honorable to be dead than to be talked to like that – I am the daughter of a jong.'

'I think you have mentioned that several times before,' I said, coldly.

She threw up her head and walked stiffly on without looking back at me. Even her little shoulders and back radiated offended dignity and stifled rage.

I glanced behind me. The mighty beast was scarce fifty feet away; ahead of us the forest was about the same distance. Duare could not see me. I stopped and faced the colossus. By the time it had dispatched me Duare would probably be close to the safety of the branches of the nearest tree.

I held my bow in one hand, but my arrows remained in the crude quiver I had fashioned to hold them behind my right shoulder. I had sense enough to realize that the only effect they might have upon this mountain of hairy sinew would be to enrage it.

After I stopped, the beast approached more slowly, almost warily. Two little eyes, set far apart, regarded me intently; two large, mulish ears pricked forward; quivering nostrils dilated.

On it came, very gradually now. A bony protuberance extending from its snout to its forehead commenced to rise until it revealed itself to my astonished gaze as an erectile horn. The member rose until it pointed forward at an angle of about forty-five degrees, a terrible weapon of offense.

I did not move. My experience of earthly animals had taught me that few will attack without provocation, and I staked my life on the chance that the same rule prevailed on Venus. But there are other provocations beside those that arouse fear or anger; a most potent one is hunger. However, this creature looked herbivorous; and I hoped that it were herbivorous. But I could not forget the basto; that somewhat resembled an American bison, yet was omnivorous.

Closer and closer came the remarkable beast, very, very slowly, as though its mind were assailed by doubts. It towered above me like a living mountain. I could feel its warm breath upon my almost naked body; but, better still, I could smell its breath – the sweet, inoffensive breath of a grass eater. My hopes rose.

The creature struck out its muzzle toward me; a low rumbling issued from its cavernous chest; that terrible horn touched me; then the cool, moist muzzle. The beast sniffed at me. Slowly the horn subsided.

Suddenly, with a snort, the animal wheeled about and went galloping off, bucking and jumping as I have seen a playful steer buck and jump, its little tail stiffly erect. It presented a most ludicrous appearance – as would a steam locomotive skipping rope. I laughed, possibly a little hysterically, for my knees were suddenly weak and wobbly. If I had not been near death, I had at least thought I was.

As I turned back toward the forest, I saw Duare standing there looking at me, and as I approached her I perceived that she was wide-eyed and trembling.

'You are very brave,' she said. Her anger seemed to have departed. 'I know that you remained there so that I might escape.'

'There really wasn't much else that I could do,' I assured her. 'And now that that's over, let's see if we can't find something to eat – something a few sizes smaller than that mountain of steaks and roasts. I think we'll go in until we strike the stream that flows through this forest. We may find a drinking place or a ford that the animals are accustimed to coming to.'

'There are many animals out there on the plain that are small,' suggested Duare. 'Why don't you hunt there?'

'There are plenty of animals, but there are not enough trees,' I replied with a laugh. 'We may need some trees in our hunting. I don't know enough about these Amtorian beasts as yet to warrant me in taking unnecessary risks,'

We moved on into the wood beneath the delicate foliage and among the strangely beautiful boles with their lacquer-like bark of white and red and yellow and blue.

Presently we came in sight of a little river winding leisurely between its violet banks, and at the same instant I saw a small creature drinking. It was about the size of a goat, but it didn't look like a goat. Its sharply pointed ears were constantly moving, as though on the alert for the slightest sound of danger; its tufted tail switched nervously. A collar of short horns encircled its neck just where it joined the head. They pointed slightly forward. There must have been a dozen of them. I could not but wonder what their specific purpose might be until I recalled the vere from whose horrible maw I had so recently escaped. That necklace of short horns would most certainly have discouraged any creature that was in the habit of swallowing its prey whole.

Very gently, I pushed Duare behind a tree and crept forward, fitting an arrow to my bow. As I was preparing to shoot, the creature threw up its head and turned half around. Probably it had heard me. I had been creeping on it from behind, but its change of position revealed its left side to me, and I planted my first arrow squarely in its heart.

So we made our camp beside the river and dined on juicy chops, delicious fruits, and the clear water from the little stream. Our surroundings were idyllic. Strange birds sang to us, arboreal quadrupeds swung through the trees jabbering melodiously in soft sing-song voices.

'It is very lovely here,' said Duare, dreamily. 'I wish that I were not the daughter of a jong.'

CHAPTER 7

THE GLOOMY CASTLE

WE WERE both loath to leave this lovely spot, and so we tarried there for two days while I made weapons for Duare and a new spear for myself.

I had constructed a little platform in a tree that overhung the river; and there at night we were comparatively safe from predatory animals, while the soft music of the purling water lulled us to sleep, a sleep that might be suddenly broken by the savage roars of hunting beasts or the screams of their victims, to which the distant lowing and bellowing of the vast herds upon the plain furnished an harmonious undertone in this raw aria of life.

It was our last night in this pleasant camp. We were sitting on our little platform watching the fish leaping and jumping in the river below.

'I could be happy here forever – with you, Duare,' I said.

'One may not think of happiness alone,' she replied; 'there is duty also.'

'But what if circumstances make us helpless to perform our duties? Aren't we warranted in making the best of our fate and making the most of the chance for happiness where we find it?'

'What do you mean?' she asked.

'I mean that there is practically no possibility that we can ever reach Vepaja. We do not know where it is, and if we did, it seems to me that there is not even the remotest chance that we should survive the dangers that must lie along the unknown trail that leads back to the house of Mintep, your father,'

'I know that you are right,' she replied a little wearily, 'but it is my duty to try; and I may never cease to seek to return, to the end of my life, no matter how remote I may know the chance of success may be.'

'Isn't that being a little unreasonable, Duare?'

'You do not understand, Carson Napier. If I had a brother or sister it might make a difference; but I have neither, and my father and I are the last of our line. It is not for myself nor for my father that I must return but for my country – the royal line of the jongs of Vepaja must not be broken, and there is none to perpetuate it but myself.'

'And if we do return – what then?'

'When I am twenty, I shall marry a noble selected by my father, and after my father dies, I shall be vadjong* until my oldest son is twenty; then he will be jong.'

'But with the longevity serum that your scientists have perfected, your father will never die; so why return?'

'I hope he will not die, but there are accidents and battles and assassins. Oh, why discuss it! The royal line must be preserved!'

'And what of me, if we reach Vepaja?' I asked.

'What do you mean?'

'Will there be a chance for me?'

'I do not understand.'

'If your father consents, will you marry me?' I blurted.

Duare flushed. 'How many times must I tell you that you may not speak of such things to me?'

'I can't help it, Duare; I love you. I care nothing for customs nor jongs nor dynasties. I shall tell your father that I love you, and I shall tell him that you love me.'

'I do not love you; you have no right to say that. It is sinful and wicked. Because once I was weak and lost my head and said a thing I did not mean, you have no right to constantly throw it in my face.'

Now that was just like a woman. I had been fighting every impulse to keep from speaking of love during all the time we had been together. I couldn't recall but one other instance when I had lost control of myself, yet she accused me of constantly throwing in her face the one admission of love that she had made.

'Well,' I said, sullenly, 'I shall do what I said I'd do, if I ever see your father again.'

'And do you know what he will do?'

'If he's the right kind of a father he'll say, "Bless you, my children." '

'He is a jong before he is a father, and he will have you destroyed. Even if you do not make any such mad admission

*Vadjong, meaning queen, is derived from vadja, female, and jong, king.

to him, I shall have to use all of my powers of persuasion to save you from death.'

'Why should he kill me?'

'No man who has spoken, without royal permission, to a janjong* is ordinarily permitted to live. That you may be with me alone for months and possibly years before we return to Vepaja will but tend to exaggerate the seriousness of the situation. I shall plead your service to me; that you risked your life innumerable times to preserve mine; and that, I think, will have sufficient weight to save you from death; but, of course, you will be banished from Vepaja.'

'That is a pleasant outlook. I may lose my life, and I am certain to lose you. Under such circumstances, do you think that I will prosecute the search for Vepaja with much enthusiasm or diligence?'

'Perhaps not with enthusiasm; but with diligence, yes. You will do it for me, because of that thing which you call love. I have learned that you will do anything for that.'

'Possibly you are right,' I said, and I knew that she was.

The next day we started, in accordance with a plan we had formulated, to follow the little river down toward the big river along which we would continue to the sea. Where we should go from there was problematical. We decided to wait until we reached the sea before making any further plans. What lay before us we could not guess; had we been able to, we might have fled back to the comparative safety of the gloomy forest we had so recently quitted with delight.

Late in the afternoon we were taking a short cut across open ground where the river made a great bend. It was rather rough going, for there were many rocks and bowlders, and the surface of the land was cut by shallow gullies. Large bowlders or outcroppings of rock were numerous and cut off our view in all directions when we were on the higher ground, while from the bottoms of the gullies we could see only a short distance ahead.

As we clambered up the bank of a particularly deep gully, I chanced to glance back and saw a strange animal standing on the opposite rim watching us. It was about the size of a German police dog, but there the similarity ceased. It had a massive, curved beak remarkably similar to that of a

*Princess.

parrot; and its body was covered with feathers; but it was no bird, for it went on four legs and had no wings. Forward of its two short ears were three horns, one in front of either ear and the third growing midway between the others. As it turned part way around to look at something we could not see, I saw that it had no tail. At a distance its legs and feet appeared bird-like.

'Do you see what I see, Duare?' I asked, nodding in the direction of the weird creature; 'or am I suffering from a touch of fever?'

'Of course I see it,' she replied, 'but I don't know what it is. I am sure that there is no such creature on the island of Vepaja.'

'There's another of them, and another, and another!' I exclaimed. 'Lord! there must be a dozen of them.'

They were standing on a little knot surveying us when suddenly the one we had first seen raised its grotesque head and voiced a hoarse, wailing scream; then it started down into the gulley and headed for us at a rapid gallop, and behind it came its fellows, all now voicing that hideous cry.

'What are we going to do?' asked Duare. 'Do you suppose they are dangerous?'

'I don't know whether they are dangerous or not,' I replied, 'but I wish that there were a tree handy.'

'A forest does have its advantages,' admitted Duare. 'What are we going to do?'

'It would do no good to run; so we might as well stand here and have it out with them. We'll have some advantage as they come up the bank of the gully.'

I fitted an arrow to my bow and Duare did likewise; then we stood waiting for them to come within range. They loped easily across the bottom of the gully and started the ascent. They didn't seem to be in much of a hurry; that is, they didn't seem to be extending themselves to their full speed, probably because we were not running away from them.

Probably this surprised them, for they presently slowed down to a walk and advanced warily. They had ceased their baying. The feathers along their backs rose stiffly erect as they slunk toward us.

Aiming carefully at the foremost, I loosed an arrow. It struck the beast full in the chest, and with a scream it stopped and tore at the feathered shaft protruding from its body. The others halted and surrounded it. They made a strange cackling sound.

The wounded creature staggered and sank to the ground, and instantly its fellows were upon it, tearing and rending. For a moment it fought fiercely to defend itself, but futilely.

As the others commenced to devour their fallen comrade I motioned Duare to follow me, and we turned and ran toward the trees we could see about a mile away where the river turned back across our line of march. But we hadn't gone far before we heard again the infernal screaming that told us that the pack was again on our trail.

This time they overtook us while we were at the bottom of a depression, and once again we made a stand. Instead of attacking us directly, the beasts slunk about just out of range, as though they knew the danger line beyond which they would be safe; then slowly they circled us until we were surrounded.

'If they charge now, all at once,' said Duare, 'we are sure to be finished.'

'Perhaps if we succeed in killing a couple of them the others will stop to devour them, thus giving us another chance to get closer to the wood,' I argued with an assumed optimism that I did not feel.

As we waited for the next move of our antagonists, we heard a loud shout in the direction from which we had come. Looking quickly up, I saw a man seated upon the back of a four-footed animal at the rim of the depression in which we stood.

At the sound of the human voice, the beasts surrounding us looked in the direction of the interruption and immediately commenced to cackle. The man on the beast rode slowly down toward us, and as he came to the ring of beasts, they moved aside and let him pass through their savage ranks.

'It is fortunate for you that I came when I did,' said the stranger, as the beast he rode stopped in front of us; 'these kazars of mine are a ferocious lot,' He was eyeing us intently, especially Duare. 'Who are you, and where are you from?' he demanded.

'We are strangers, and we are lost,' I replied. 'I am from California.' I did not wish to tell him that we were from

Vepaja until we knew more of him. If he were a Thorist, he was an enemy; and the less he knew about us the better, especially that we were from the country of Mintep, the jong, than whom the Thorists have no more bitter enemy, nor any they hate more venomously.

'California,' he repeated. 'I never heard of such a country. Where is it?'

'In North America,' I replied, but he only shook his head. 'And who are you?' I asked, 'and what country is this?'

'This is Noobol, but that of course you must already know. This part of it is known as Morov. I am Skor, the jong of Morov. But you have not told me your names.'

'This is Duare,' I replied, 'and I am Carson.' I did not give my surname, as they are seldom used on Venus.

'And where were you going?'

'We were trying to find our way to the sea.'

'From where did you come?'

'Recently we were in Kapdor,' I explained.

I saw his eyes narrow ominously. 'So you are Thorists!' he snapped.

'No,' I assured him, 'we are not. We were prisoners of the Thorists.' I hoped that my guess had been a good one and that he was not kindly disposed toward the Thorists. The slender thread upon which I hung my hopes was no more substantial than the frown that had clouded his brow at my admission that we had just come from Kapdor.

To my relief his expression changed. 'I am glad that you are not Thorists; otherwise I would not help you. I have no use for the breed.'

'You will help us, then?' I asked.

'With pleasure,' he replied. He was looking at Duare as he spoke, and I did not exactly relish the tone of his voice nor the expression on his face.

The kazars were circling around us, cackling and whistling. When one of them approached us too close, Skor would flick it with the lash of a long whip he carried; and the creature would retreat, screaming and cackling the louder.

'Come', he said presently, 'I will take you to my house; then we may discuss plans for the future. The woman may ride behind me on my zorat; you may walk. It is not far.'

'I prefer to walk,' said Duare. 'I am accustomed to it now.'

Skor's eyes narrowed a bit. He started to speak, and then he checked himself. Finally he shrugged. 'As you will,' he said, and turned the head of his mount back in the direction from which he had come.

The creature he rode, which he called a zorat, was unlike any beast that I had ever seen before. It was about the size of a small horse. Its long, slender legs suggested great speed. Its feet were round and nailless and heavily calloused on the bottoms. Its almost vertical pasterns suggested that it might be a hard-gaited beast, but this was not so. Later I learned that almost horizontal femurs and humeri absorbed the jolts and rendered the zorat an easy-riding saddle animal.

Above its withers and just forward of its kidneys were soft pads or miniature humps which formed a perfect saddle with natural pommel and cantel. Its head was short and broad, with two large, saucer-like eyes and pendulous ears. Its teeth were those of a herbivore. Its only means of defense seemed to lie in its fleetness, although, as I afterward had occasion to discover, it can use its jaws and teeth most effectively when its short temper is aroused.

We walked beside Skor on the journey toward his house, the grotesque kazars following docilely behind at the command of their master. The way led toward the great bend of the river, that we had sought to avoid by taking a short cut, and a forest that lined its banks. The proximity of the kazars made me nervous, for occasionally one of them would trot close at our heels; and I was fearful that Duare might be injured by one of the fierce beasts before I could prevent it. I asked Skor what purpose the creatures served.

'I use them for hunting,' he replied, 'but principally for protection. I have enemies; and then, too, there are many savage beasts roaming at large in Morov. The kazars are quite fearless and very savage fighters. Their greatest weakness is their predilection for cannibalism; they will abandon a fight to devour one of their own number that has fallen.'

Shortly after we entered the forest we came upon a large, gloomy, fortress-like building of stone. It was built upon a low rise of ground at the water's edge, the river lapping the masonry upon that side. A stone wall connecting with the river wall of the building enclosed several acres of clear land in front of the structure. A heavy gate closed the only aperture that was visible in this wall.

As we approached, Skor shouted, 'Open! It is the jong,' and the gates swung slowly outward.

As we entered, several armed men, who had been sitting beneath one of the several trees that had been left standing when the ground was cleared, arose and stood with bowed heads. They were a hard and also a sad looking lot. The feature that struck me most forcibly was the strange hue of their skin, a repulsive, unhealthy pallor, a seeming bloodlessness. I caught the eyes of one that chanced to raise his head as we passed, and I shivered. They were glazed, clammy eyes, without light, without fire. I would have thought the fellow stone blind but for the fact that the instant that my eyes caught his they dropped swiftly. Another had an ugly, open wound across his cheek from temple to chin; it gaped wide, but it did not bleed.

Skor snapped a brief order; and two of the men herded the pack of cackling kazars into a strong enclosure built beside the gateway, as we proceeded on toward the house. Perhaps I should call it a castle, for that is what it most resembled.

The enclosure across which we passed was barren except for the few trees that had been left standing. It was littered with refuse of all descriptions and was unspeakably disorderly and untidy. Old sandals, rags, broken pottery, and the garbage from the castle kitchens were strewn promiscuously about. The only spot from which any effort had been made to remove the litter was a few hundred square feet of stone flagging before the main entrance to the building.

Here Skor dismounted as three more men similar to those at the gate came lifelessly from the interior of the building. One of these took Skor's mount and led it away, the others stood one on either side of the entrance as we passed in.

The doorway was small, the door that closed it thick and heavy. It seemed to be the only opening on the first floor on this side of the castle. Along the second and third floor levels I had seen small windows heavily barred. At one corner of the building I had noticed a tower rising two more stories above the main part of the castle. This, too, had small windows, some of which were barred.

The interior of the building was dark and gloomy. Coupled with the appearance of the inmates I had already seen it engendered within me a feeling of depression that I could not throw off.

'You must be hungry,' suggested Skor. 'Come out into the inner court – it is pleasanter there – and I will have food served.'

We followed him down a short corridor and through a doorway into a courtyard around which the castle was built. The enclosure reminded me of a prison yard. It was flagged with stone. No living thing grew there. The grey stone walls, cut with their small windows, rose upon four sides. There had been no effort toward architectural ornamentation in the design of the structure, nor any to beautify the courtyard in any way. Here, too, was litter and trash that it had evidently been easier to throw into the inner court than carry to the outer.

I was oppressed by forebodings of ill. I wished that we had never entered the place, but I tried to brush my fears aside. I argued that Skor had given no indications of being other than a kindly and solicitous host. He had seemed anxious to befriend us. That he was a jong I had commenced to doubt, for there was no suggestion of royalty in his entourage or his mode of living.

In the center of the court a plank table was flanked by grimy, well-worn benches. On the table were the remains of a meal. Skor graciously waved us toward the benches; then he clapped his hands together three times before he seated himself at the head of the table.

'I seldom have guests here,' he said. 'It is quite a pleasant treat for me. I hope that you will enjoy your stay. I am sure that I shall,' and as he spoke he looked at Duare in that way that I did not like.

'I am sure that we might enjoy it could we remain,' replied Duare quickly, 'but that is not possible. I must return to the house of my father.'

'Where is that?' asked Skor.

'In Vepaja,' explained Duare.

'I never heard of that country,' said Skor. 'Where is it?'

'You never heard of Vepaja!' exclaimed Duare incredulously. 'Why, all the present country of Thora was called Vepaja until the Thorists rose and took it and drove the remnants of the ruling class to the island that is now all that remains of ancient Vepaja.'

'Oh, yes, I had heard of that,' admitted Skor; 'but it was a long time ago and in distant Trabol.'

'Is this not Trabol?' asked Duare.

'No,' replied Skor; 'this is Strabol.'

'But Strabol is the hot country,' argued Duare. 'No one can live in Strabol.'

'You are in Strabol now. It is hot here during a portion of the year but not so hot as to be unendurable.'

I was interested. If what Skor said were true, we had crossed the equator and were now in the northern hemisphere of Venus. The Vepajans had told me that Strabol was uninhabitable – a steaming jungle reeking with heat and moisture and inhabited only by fierce and terrible beasts and reptiles. The entire northern hemisphere was a *terra incognita* to the men of the southern hemisphere, and for that reason I had been anxious to explore it.

With the responsibility of Duare on my shoulders I could not do much exploring, but I might learn something from Skor; so I asked him of the country farther north.

'It is no good,' he snapped. 'It is a land of fools. They frown upon true science and progress. They drove me out; they would have killed me. I came here and established the kingdom of Morov. That was many years ago – perhaps a hundred years. I have never returned since to the country of my birth; but sometimes their people come here,' and he laughed unpleasantly.

Just then a woman came from the building, evidently in response to Skor's summons. She was middle-aged. Her skin was the same repulsive hue as that of the men I had seen, and it was very dirty. Her mouth hung open and her tongue protruded; it was dry and swollen. Her eyes were glazed and staring. She moved with a slow, awkward shuffle. And now, behind her, came two men. They were much as she; there was something indescribably revolting about all three.

'Take these away!' snapped Skor with a wave of the hand toward the soiled dishes. 'And bring food.'

The three gathered up the dishes and shuffled away. None of them spoke. The look of horror in Duare's eyes could not have gone unnoticed by Skor.

'You do not like my retainers?' demanded Skor testily.

'But I said nothing,' objected Duare.

'I saw it in your face.' Suddenly Skor broke into laughter. There was no mirth in it, nor was there laughter in his eyes but another expression, a terrible glint that passed as quickly as it had come. 'They are excellent servants,' he said in normal tones; 'they do not talk too much, and *they do whatever I tell them to do*.'

Presently the three returned carrying vessels of food. There was meat, partially raw, partially burned, and wholly unpalatable; there were fruits and vegetables, none of which appeared to have been washed; there was wine. It was the only thing there fit for human consumption.

The meal was not a success. Duare could not eat. I sipped my wine and watched Skor eating ravenously of all the filthy mess. From a partially open doorway several small animals came scurrying across the flagging toward the table. Skor flung them a bone upon which he had been gnawing, and they commenced to fight for it while Skor looked on laughing. These creatures were rodents about the size of earthly house cats.

I saw Duare surreptitiously removing the food from her plate and dropping it on the floor when Skor was not looking at her. Following her strategy, I did the same. Thus we avoided eating the food without offending our host, and the mistals had a hearty meal.

Darkness was falling as Skor arose from the table. 'I will show you to your rooms,' he said. 'You must be tired.' His tone and manner were those of the perfect host. 'Tomorrow you shall set out again upon your journey.'

Relieved by this promise, we followed him into the house. It was a dark and gloomy abode, chill and cheerless. We followed him up a stairway to the second floor and into a long, dark corridor. Presently he stopped before a door and threw it open.

'May you sleep well,' he said to Duare, bowing and motioning her to enter.

Silently Duare crossed the threshold and Skor closed the door behind her; then he conducted me to the end of the corridor, up two flights of stairs and ushered me into a circular room that I guessed was in the tower I had seen when we entered the castle's outer courtyard.

'I hope you awaken refreshed,' he said politely and withdrew, closing the door behind him.

I heard his footsteps descending the stairs until they were lost in the distance. I thought of Duare down there alone in this gloomy and mysterious pile. I had no reason to believe that she was not safe, but nevertheless I was apprehensive. Anyway, I had no intention of leaving her alone down there. If anything *should* happen, I wanted to be where I could protect her.

I waited until Skor had had plenty of time to go to his own quarters wherever they might be; then I stepped to the door, determined to go to Duare. I laid my hand upon the latch and sought to open it. It was locked from the outside. Quickly I went to the several windows. Each was heavily barred. Faintly from the distant recesses of that forbidding pile I thought I heard a mocking laugh.

CHAPTER 8

The Girl in the Tower

The tower room in which I found myself imprisoned was lighted only by the mysterious night glow that relieves the nocturnal darkness of Venus, that must otherwise have been impenetrable. Dimly I saw the furnishings of the room – they were meager. The place had more the aspect of a prison cell than a guest chamber.

I crossed to a chest of drawers and investigated it. It was filled with odds and ends of worn and useless apparel, bits of string, a few lengths of rope. I paced the floor worrying about Duare. I was helpless. I could do nothing. It would be vain to pound upon the door or call for release. The will that had incarcerated me was supreme here. Only by the voluntary act of that will could I be released.

Seating myself on a rude bench before a small table I tried to plan; I sought to discover some loophole for escape. Apparently there was none. I arose and once again examined the window bars and the sturdy door; they were impregnable.

Finally I crossed to a rickety couch that stood against the wall and lay down upon the worn and odorous hide that covered it. Absolute silence reigned – the silence of the tomb. For a long time it was unbroken; then I heard a sound above me. I listened, trying to interpret it. It was like the slow padding of naked feet – back and forth, to and fro above my head.

I had thought that I was on the top floor of the tower, but now I realized that there must be another room above the one in which I had been placed – if the sound I heard was that of human feet.

Listening to that monotonous padding had a soporific effect upon my jaded nerves. I caught myself dozing a couple of times. I did not wish to go to sleep; something seemed to warn me that I must remain awake, but at last I must have succumbed.

How long I slept I do not know. I awoke with a start, conscious that something touched me. A dim figure was leaning over me. I started to rise. Instantly strong fingers clutched my throat – cold, clammy fingers – the fingers of Death they seemed.

Struggling, I sought the throat of my antagonist. I closed upon it – it, too, was cold and clammy. I am a strong man, but the *thing* upon my chest was stronger. I struck at it with closed fists. From the doorway came a low, hideous laugh. I felt my scalp stiffen to the horror of it all.

I sensed that death was close, and a multitude of thoughts raced through my mind. But uppermost among them were thoughts of Duare and harrowing regret that I must leave her here in the clutches of the fiend I was now certain was the instigator of this attack upon me. I guessed that its purpose was to dispose of me and thus remove the only possible obstacle that might stand between himself and Duare, whom he evidently desired.

I was still struggling when something struck me on the head; then came oblivion.

*

It was daylight when I regained consciousness. I still lay upon the couch, sprawled upon my back. Staring up at the ceiling, trying to collect my thoughts and memories, I perceived a crack just above me such as might have been made by a trap door partially raised; and through the crack two eyes were peering down at me.

Some new horror? I did not move. I lay there fascinated, watching the trap door slowly open. Presently a face was revealed. It was the face of a girl, a very beautiful girl; but it was strained and drawn and the eyes were terrified, frightened eyes.

In a whisper, the girl spoke. 'You are alive?' she asked.

I raised myself on an elbow. 'Who are you?' I demanded. 'Is this some new trick to torture me?'

'No. I am a prisoner, too. He has gone away. Perhaps we can escape.'

'How?' I asked. I was still skeptical, believing her a confederate of Skor.

'Can you get up here? There are no bars on my windows; that is because they are so high that no one could jump from them without being killed or badly injured. If we only had a rope!'

I considered the matter for a moment before I replied. What if it were a trick after all? Could I be any worse off in one room in this accursed castle than in another?

'There is rope down here,' I said. 'I will get it and come up. Perhaps there is not enough to be of any use to us, but I will bring what there is,'

'How will you get up?' she asked.

'That will not be difficult. Wait until I get the rope.'

I went to the chest of drawers and took out all the rope and string that I had discovered there the previous night; then I shoved the chest across the floor until it was directly beneath the trap door.

From the top of the chest I could easily reach the edge of the floor above. Handing the rope up to the girl, I quickly drew myself up into the room with her; then she closed the trap and we stood facing one another.

Despite her dishevelled and frightened appearance, I found her even more beautiful than I had at first thought her; and as her fine eyes met mine in mutual appraisement, my fears of treachery vanished. I was sure that no duplicity lurked behind that lovely countenance.

'You need not doubt me,' she said as though she had read my thoughts, 'though I cannot wonder that you doubt every one in this terrible place.'

'Then how can you trust me?' I asked. 'You know nothing of me.'

'I know enough,' she replied. 'From that window I saw you when you and your companion came yesterday with Skor, and I knew that he had two more victims. I heard them bring you to the room below last night. I did not know which one of you it was. I wanted to warn you then, but am so afraid of Skor. I walked the floor for a long time trying to decide what to do.'

'Then it was you I heard walking?'

'Yes. Then I heard them come again; I heard sounds of a scuffle and Skor's awful laugh. Oh, how I hate and fear that laugh! After that it was quiet. I thought they had killed you, if it were you, or taken the girl away, if it were she whom they had imprisoned in the room below. Oh, the poor thing! and she is so beautiful. I hope she got away safely, but I am afraid there can be little hope of that.'

'Got away? What do you mean?' I demanded.

'She escaped very early this morning. I do not know how she got out of her room, but from the window I saw her cross the outer courtyard. She climbed the wall on the river side, and she must have dropped into the river. I did not see her again.'

'Duare has escaped! You are sure it was she?'

'It was the beautiful girl who came here with you yesterday. About an hour after she got away, Skor must have discovered that she was gone. He came out of the castle in a terrible rage. He took with him all of the miserable creatures that watch the gate, and all his fierce kazars, and set out in pursuit. Possibly never again may we have such an opportunity to escape.'

'Let's get busy ,then,' I exclaimed. 'Have you a plan?'

'Yes,' she replied. 'With the rope we can lower ourselves to the castle roof and from there to the courtyard. There is no one watching the gate; the kazars are gone; if we are discovered, we shall have to trust to our legs. But there are only three or four of Skor's retainers left in the castle, and they are not very alert when he is not there.'

'I have my weapons,' I reminded her. 'Skor did not take them away from me, and if any of his people try to stop is I will kill them.'

She shook her head. 'You cannot kill them,' she whispered, shuddering.

'What do you mean?' I demanded. 'Why can I not kill them?'

'Because they are already dead.' She whispered the words fearfully.

I looked at her in astonishment as slowly the meaning of her words filtered to my shocked brain to explain the pitiful creatures that had filled me with such disgust on the previous day.

'But,' I exclaimed, 'how can they be dead? I saw them move about and obey the commands of Skor.'

'I do not know,' she replied; 'it is Skor's terrible secret. Presently you will be as they, if we do not escape; and the girl who came with you, and I – after a while. He will keep us a little longer in the flesh for the purpose of his experiments. Every day he takes a little blood from me. He is seeking the secret of life. He says that he can reproduce body cells, and with these he has instilled synthetic life into the poor creatures that he has resurrected from the grave. But it is only a parody on life; no blood flows in those dead veins, and the dead minds are animated only by the thoughts that Skor transmits to them by some occult, telepathic means.

'But what he most desires is the power to reproduce germ cells and thus propagate a new race of beings fashioned according to his own specifications. That is why he takes blood from me; that is why he wanted the girl you call Duare. When our blood has become so depleted that death is near, he will kill us and we will be like these others. But he would not keep us here; he would take us to the city where he rules as jong. Here he keeps only a few poor, degraded specimens; but he says that in Kormor he has many fine ones.'

'So he *is* a jong? I doubted it.'

'He made himself a jong and created his own subjects,' she said.

'And he kept you only to draw blood from you?'

'Yes. He is not like other men; he is not human.'

'How long have you been here?'

'A long time; but I am still alive because Skor has been away most of the time in Kormor.'

'Well, we must get away, too, before he returns. I want to search for Duare. She will be helpless out there alone.'

I went to one of the windows, none of which was barred, and looked down on the castle roof below, a distance of about twenty feet; then I got the rope and examined it carefully. There were several pieces, in all about forty feet – more than enough; also it was stout rope. I tied the pieces together and then returned to the window. The girl was at my elbow.

'Can any one see us from here?' I asked.

'The creatures are not very alert,' she replied. 'Those that Skor left here are the servants. They remain in a room on the first floor on the other side of the castle. When he is away, they just sit. After a while two of them will bring food for us; and we should get away before they come, for sometimes they forget to go back to their quarters; then they sit around outside my door for hours. You will notice that there is a grille in the door; they would see us if we attempted to escape while they were there.'

'We'll start now,' I said. Then I made a loop in one end of the rope and passed it around the girl's body so that she could sit in it while I lowered her to the roof.

Without an instant's hesitation she stepped to the sill of the window and lowered herself over the edge until she was seated securely in the loop. Bracing my feet against the wall, I let her down rapidly until I felt the rope go slack in my hands.

I then dragged her cot close beneath the window, passed the free end of the rope beneath it and out the window, letting it fall toward the roof below. This gave me two strands of rope reaching to the roof with the middle part of the rope passing around the cot which was too large to be dragged through the window by my weight as I descended.

Grasping both strands firmly in my two hands, I slipped through the window and slid quickly to the side of the waiting girl; then I pulled in rapidly on one end of the rope, dragging the free end around the cot until it fell to the roof. Thus I retrieved the rope for use in descending the remainder of the way to the ground.

We crossed the roof quickly to the edge overlooking the outer courtyard into which we expected to descend. There was no one in sight, and I was just about to lower the girl over the edge when a loud shout from behind us startled us both.

Turning, we saw three of Skor's creatures looking at us from an upper window of the castle on the opposite side of the inner court. Almost as we turned, the three left the window, and we could hear them shouting through the castle.

'What shall we do!' cried the girl. 'We are lost! They will come to the roof by the tower door, and they will have us trapped. They were not the servants; they were three of his armed men. I thought they had all accompanied him, but I was wrong,.'

I said nothing, but I seized her hand and started toward the far end of the castle roof. A sudden hope had flared within me, born of an idea suggested by what the girl had told me of Duare's escape.

We ran as fast as we could, and when we reached the edge, we looked down upon the river lapping the castle wall two stories below. I passed the rope about the girl's waist. She asked no question; she made no comment. Quickly she climbed over the low parapet, and I commenced lowering her toward the river below.

Hideous mouthings arose behind me. I turned and saw three dead men running toward me across the roof. Then I lowered away so rapidly that the rope burned my fingers, but there was no time to lose. I feared that they would be upon me before I could lower the girl to the dubious safety of the swirling waters.

Nearer and nearer sounded the hurrying footsteps and the incoherent yammerings of the corpses. I heard a splash, and the rope went slack in my fingers. I glanced behind. The nearest of the creatures was already extending his hands to seize me. It was one of those that I had noticed at the gate the day before; I recognized it by the bloodless gash across its cheek. Its dead eyes were expressionless – glazed and staring – but its mouth was contorted in a ghastly snarl.

Immediate recapture faced me; there was but a single alternative. I sprang to the top of the parapet and leaped. I had always been a good diver, but I doubt that I ever made a prettier swan dive in my life than I did that day from the parapet of the gloomy castle of Skor, the jong of Morov.

As I rose to the surface of the river, shaking the water from my eyes, I looked about for the girl; she was nowhere to be seen. I knew that she could not have reached the river bank in the short time that had elapsed since I had lowered her into the water, for the masonry of the castle and the walls which extended both above and below the building offered not even a hand hold for hundreds of feet in both directions, and the opposite shore was too far away.

As I cast about me in all directions as the current carried me down stream, I saw her head rise above the surface of the water a short distance below me. Swiftly I struck out for her. She went down again just before I reached her, but I dived for her and brought her to the surface. She was still conscious but almost out. She lay very limp.

Glancing back at the castle, I saw that my would-be captors had disappeared from the roof; and I guessed that they would shortly appear on the bank of the river ready to seize us when we emerged. But I had no intention of emerging on their side.

Dragging the girl with me, I struck out for the opposite shore. The river here was considerably deeper and broader than at the point we had first encountered it farther up stream. Now it was quite a river. What strange creatures inhabited its depths I had no means of knowing. I could only hope that if any were large and carnivorous none such would discover us.

The girl lay very quiet; she did not struggle at all. I began to fear that she was dead, and so I exerted myself still more to reach the bank quickly. The current bore us down stream; and I was glad of that, for it was taking us farther away from the castle and retainers of Skor.

At last I reached the bank and dragged the girl out onto a little patch of pale violet grass and set to work to resuscitate her, but even as I commenced she opened her eyes and looked up at me. A shadow of a smile touched her lips.

'I shall be all right in a minute,' she said weakly. 'I was so frightened.'

'Don't you know how to swim?' I asked.

She shook her head. 'No.'

'And you let me lower you into the river without telling me!' I was amazed by the sheer bravery of her act.

'There was nothing else to be done,' she said simply. 'Had I told you, you would not have lowered me, and we both should have been recaptured. I do not see even now how you got down before they seized you.'

'I dived,' I explained.

'You jumped from the top of that castle? It is incredible!'

'You do not come from a land where there is much water,' I commented with a laugh.

'What makes you think so?'

'If you did, you would have seen enough diving to know that mine was nothing extraordinary.'

'My country is in a mountainous district,' she admitted, 'where the streams are torrents and there is little swimming.'

'And where is that?' I asked.

'Oh, it is very far,' she replied. 'I do not even know where.'

'How did you happen to get into Skor's country?'

'During a war in my country I was captured with others by the enemy. They carried us down out of the mountains into a great plain. One night two of us escaped. My companion was a soldier who had been long in the service of my father. He was very loyal. He tried to return me to my country, but we became lost. I do not know how long we wandered, but at last we came to a great river.

'Here were people who went in boats upon the river. They lived in the boats always, fishing. They sought to capture us, and my companion was killed defending me; then they took me. But I was not with them long. The first night several men were quarreling over me; each of them claimed me as his own. And while they quarreled, I slipped into a small boat tied to the larger one and floated away down the great river.

'I drifted for many days and nearly starved to death, although I saw fruits and nuts growing along the banks of the river. But the boat was without oars and was so heavy that I could not bring it into shore across the swift current.

'Finally it ran aground by itself on a sand bar where the river ran slowly about a great bend, and it chanced that Skor was hunting near and saw me. That is all. I have been here a long time.'

CHAPTER 9

The Pygmies

As the girl finished her story, I saw the three dead men standing upon the opposite bank. For a moment they hesitated, and then they plunged into the river.

I seized the girl by the hand and raised her to her feet. Our only defense lay in flight. Although I had had to abandon my spear, I had saved my bow and arrows, the latter being tied securely in my quiver, while the former I had looped across one shoulder before leaving the tower; but of what use were arrows against dead men?

Casting another glance towards our pursuers, I saw them floundering in the deep water of the channel, and it became immediately evident that none of them could swim. They were bobbing around helplessly as the current swept them down stream. Sometimes they floated on their backs, sometimes on their faces; most of the time their heads were under water.

'We haven't much to fear from them,' I said; 'they will all drown.'

'They cannot drown,' replied the girl, with a shudder.

'I hadn't thought of that,' I admitted, 'but at least there is little likelihood that they will reach this shore; certainly not before they have been carried a long distance down stream. We shall have plenty of time to escape them.'

'Then let's be going. I hate this place. I want to get away from it.'

'I cannot go away until I have found Duare,' I told her. 'I must search for her.'

'Yes, that is right; we must try to find her. But where shall we look?'

'She would try to reach the big river and follow it to the sea,' I explained; 'and I think that she would reason much as we would, that it would be safer to follow this stream down to the larger one inasmuch as then she would have the concealing protection of the forest.'

'We shall have to keep careful watch for the dead men.'

cautioned the girl. 'If they wash ashore on this side, we shall be sure to meet them.'

'Yes; and I want to make sure where they do come ashore, because I intend crossing over and hunting for Duare on the other side.'

For some time we moved cautiously down stream in silence, both constantly alert for any sound that might portend danger. My mind was filled with thoughts of Duare and apprehension for her safety, yet occasionally it reverted to the girl at my side; and I could not but recall her courage during our escape and her generous willingness to delay her own flight that we might search for Duare. It was apparent that her character formed a trinity of loveliness with her form and her face. And I did not even know her name!

That fact struck me as being as remarkable as that I had only known her for an hour. So intimate are the bonds of mutual adversity and danger that it seemed I had known her always, that that hour was indeed an eternity.

'Do you know,' I asked, turning toward her, 'that we do not know one another's name?' and then I told her mine.

'Carson Napier!' she repeated. 'That is a strange name.'

'And what is yours?'

'Nalte voo jan kum Baltoo,' she replied, which means Nalte, the daughter of Baltoo. 'The people call me Voo Jan (The Daughter), but my friends call me Nalte.'

'And which am I to call you?' I asked.

She looked at me in surprise. 'Why, Nalte, of course.'

'I am honored by being included among your friends.'

'But are you not my best, my only friend now in all Amtor?'

I had to admit that her reasoning was sound, since as far as all the rest of Amtor was concerned, we were the only two people on that cloud-dirt planet, and we were certainly not enemies.

We were moving cautiously along within sight of the river when Nalte suddenly touched my arm and pointed toward the opposite bank, at the same time dragging me down behind a shrub.

Just opposite us a corpse had washed ashore; and a short distance below, two others. They were our pursuers. As we watched, they slowly crawled to their feet; then the one we had first seen called to the others, who presently joined him. The three corpses talked together, pointing and gesticulating. It was horrible. I felt my skin creep.

What would they do? Would they continue the search, or would they return to the castle? If the former, they would have to cross the river; and they must already have learned that there was little likelihood of their being able to do that. But that was attributing to dead brains the power to reason! It seemed incredible. I asked Nalte what she thought about it, for she knew more about them than I.

'It is a mystery to me,' she replied. 'They converse, and they appear to reason. At first I thought they were motivated through the hypnotic influence of Skor's mind solely – that they thought his thoughts, as it were; but they take independent action when Skor is away, as you have seen them do today, which refutes that theory. Skor says that they do reason. He has stimulated their nervous systems into the semblance of life, though no blood flows in their veins; but the past experiences of their lives before they died are less potent in influencing their judgments than the new system of conduct and ethics that Skor has instilled into their dead brains. He admits that the specimens he has at the castle are very dull; but that, he insists, is because they were dull people in life.'

The dead men conversed for some time and then started slowly up river in the direction of the castle, and it was with a sigh of relief that we saw them disappear.

'Now we must try to find a good place to cross,' I said. 'I wish to search the other side for some sign of Duare. She must have left footprints in the soft earth.'

'There is a ford somewhere down river,' said Nalte. 'When Skor captured me, we crossed it on our way to the castle. I do not know just where it is, but it cannot be far.'

We had descended the river some two miles from the point at which we had seen the dead men emerge upon the opposite bank, without seeing any sign of a crossing, when I heard faintly a familiar cackling that seemed to come from across the river and farther down.

'Do you hear that?' I asked Nalte. I was sure that I recognized it.

She listened intently for a moment as the cackling grew louder. 'Yes,' she replied, 'the kazars. We had better hide.'

Acting upon Nalte's suggestion we concealed ourselves behind a clump of underbrush and waited. The cackling grew in volume, and we knew that the kazars were approaching.

'Do you suppose that it is Skor's pack?' I asked.

'It must be,' she replied. 'There is no other pack in this vicinity, according to Skor.'

'Nor any wild kazars?'

'No. He says that there are no wild ones on this side of the big river. They range on the opposite side. These must be Skor's.'

We waited in silence as the sounds approached, and presently we saw the new leader of the pack trot into view on the opposite bank. Behind him strung several more of the grotesque beasts, and then came Skor, mounted on his zorat, with the dead men that formed his retinue surrounding him.

'Duare is not there!' whispered Nalte. 'Skor did not recapture her.'

We watched Skor and his party until they had passed out of sight among the trees of the forest on the other side of the river, and it was with a sigh of relief that I saw what I hoped would be the last of the jong of Morov.

While I was relieved to know that Duare had not been recaptured, I was still but little less apprehensive concerning her fate. Many dangers might beset her, alone and unprotected, in this savage land; and I had only the vaguest conception of where to search for her.

After the passing of Skor we had continued on down the river, and presently Nalte pointed ahead to a line of ripples that stretched from bank to bank where the river widened.

'There is the ford,' she said, 'but there is no use crossing it to look for Duare's trail. If she had escaped on that side of the river, the kazars would have found her before now. The fact that they didn't find her is fairly good proof that she was never over there.'

I was not so sure of that. I did not know that Duare could swim nor that she could not, but the chances were highly in favour of the latter possibility, since Duare had been born and reared in the tree city of Kooaad a thousand feet or more above the ground. Yet I could not understand why the kazar pack had not picked up her trail.

'Perhaps they found her and killed her,' I suggested, horrified at the very thought of such a tragedy.

'No,' dissented Nalte. 'Skor would have prevented that; he wanted her.'

'But something else might have killed her; they might have found her dead body.'

'Skor would have brought it back with him and invested it with the synthetic life that animates his retinue of dead,' argued Nalte.

Still I was not convinced. 'How do the kazars trail?' I asked. 'Do they follow the spoor of their quarry by scent?'

Nalte shook her head. 'Their sense of smell is extremely poor, but their vision is acute. In trailing, they depend wholly upon their eyes.'

'Then it is possible that they might not have crossed Duare's trail at all and so missed her.'

'Possible but not probable,' replied Nalte. 'What is quite probable is that she was killed and devoured by some beast before Skor was able to recapture her.'

That explanation had already occurred to me, but I did not wish to even think about it. 'Nevertheless,' I said, 'we might as well cross over to the other bank. If we are going to follow the big river down stream we shall have to cross this affluent sooner or later, and we may not find another ford as it grows broader and deeper toward its mouth.'

The ford was broad and well marked by ripples; so we had no difficulty in following it toward the opposite bank. However, we were compelled to keep our eyes on the water most of the time, as the ford took two curves that formed a flattened S, and it would have been quite easy to have stepped off into deep water and been swept down stream had we not been careful.

The result of our constant watchfulness approached disaster as we neared the left bank of the stream. The merest chance caused me to look up. I was slightly in advance of Nalte, as we walked hand in hand for greater safety. I stopped so suddenly at what I saw that the girl bumped into me. Then she looked up, and a little, involuntary cry of alarm burst from her lips.

'What are they?' she asked.

'I don't know,' I replied; 'don't you?'

'No; I never saw such creatures before. How horrid they are!'

At the edge of the water, awaiting us, were half a dozen manlike creatures, while others like them were coming from the forest, dropping from the trees to shuffle awkwardly toward the ford. They were about three feet tall and entirely covered with long hair. At first I thought that they were monkeys, although they bore a startling resemblance to human beings; but when they saw that we had discovered them, one of them spoke, and the simian theory was exploded.

'I am Ul,' said the speaker. 'Go away from the land of Ul. I am Ul; I kill!'

'We will not harm you,' I replied. 'We only want to pass through your country.'

'Go away!' growled Ul, baring sharp fighting fangs.

By now, fifty of the fierce little men were gathered at the water's edge, growling, menacing. They were without clothing or ornaments and carried no weapons, but their sharp fangs and the bulging muscles of their shoulders and arms bespoke their ability to carry out Ul's threats.

'What are we going to do?' demanded Nalte. 'They will tear us to pieces the moment that we step out of the water.'

'Perhaps I can persuade them to let us pass,' I said, but after five minutes of fruitless effort I had to admit defeat. Ul's only reply to my arguments was, 'Go away! I kill! I kill!'

I hated to turn back, for I knew that we must cross the river eventually; and we might not find such another crossing; but at last, reluctantly, I retraced my steps to the right bank hand in hand with Nalte. As we reached the shore, we glanced back; there stood the little, hairy men watching us in silence; then we turned into the forest and saw them no more.

All the remainder of the day I searched for traces of Duare as we followed the course of the river downward, but my efforts were without success. I was disheartened. I felt that I should never see her again. Nalte tried to cheer me up, but inasmuch as she believed that Duare was dead, she was not very successful.

Late in the afternoon I succeeded in killing a small animal.

As we had eaten nothing all that day, we were both famished; so we soon had a fire going and were grilling cuts of the tender meat.

After we had eaten, I built a rude platform among the branches of a large tree and gathered a number of huge leaves to serve as mattress and covering, and as darkness fell Nalte and I settled ourselves, not uncomfortably, in our lofty sanctuary.

For a while we were silent, each wrapped in his own thoughts. I do not know about Nalte's, but mine were gloomy enough. I cursed the day that I had conceived the idea to build the huge torpedo that had carried me from Earth to Venus, and in the next thought I blessed it because it had made it possible for me to know and to love Duare.

It was Nalte who broke the silence. As though she had read my thoughts, she said, 'You loved Duare very much.'

'Yes,' I replied.

Nalte sighed. 'It must be sad to lose one's mate.'

'She was not my mate.'

'Not your mate?' Nalte's tone expressed her surprise. 'But you loved one another?'

'Duare did not love me,' I replied. 'At least she said she didn't. You see, she was the daughter of a jong; and she couldn't love any one until after she was twenty.'

Nalte laughed. 'Love does not come or go in accordance with any laws or customs,' she said.

'But even if Duare had loved me, which she didn't, she couldn't have said so; she couldn't even talk of love because she was the daughter of a jong and too young. I don't understand it, of course, but that is because I am from another world and know nothing of your customs.'

'I am nineteen,' said Nalte; 'and the daughter of a jong, but if I loved a man I should say so.'

'Perhaps the customs of your country and those of Duare's are not the same,' I suggested.

'They must be very different,' agreed Nalte, 'for in my country a man does not speak to a girl of love until she has told him that she loves him; and the daughter of the jong chooses her own mate whenever she pleases.'

'That custom may have its advantages,' I admitted, 'but if I loved a girl, I should want the right to tell her so.'

'Oh, the men find ways of letting a girl know without putting it into words. I could tell if a man loved me, but if I loved him very much I wouldn't wait for that.'

'And what if he didn't love you?' I asked.

Nalte tossed her head. 'I'd make him.'

I could readily understand that Nalte might be a very difficult young person not to love, if you gather what I mean from my clumsy exposition. She was slender and dark, with an olive skin and a mass of black hair in lovely disorder. Her eyes sparkled with health and intelligence. Her features were regular and almost boyish, and over all was the suggestion of a veil of dignity that bespoke her blood. I could not doubt but that she was the daughter of a jong. It seemed to be my fate to encounter daughters of jongs. I said as much to Nalte.

'How many have you met?' she asked.

'Two,' I replied, 'you and Duare.'

'That is not very many when you consider how many jongs there must be in Amtor, and how many daughters they must have. My father has seven.'

'Are they all as lovely as you?' I asked.

'Do you think me lovely?'

'You know you are.'

'But I like to hear people say so. I like to hear you say it,' she added softly.

The roars of hunting beasts came up to us from the dim forest aisles, the screams of stricken prey; then the silence of the night broken only by the murmuring of the river rolling down to some unknown sea.

I was considering a tactful reply to Nalte's ingenuous observation when I dozed and fell asleep.

I felt some one shaking me by the shoulder. I opened my eyes to look up into Nalte's. 'Are you going to sleep all day?' she demanded, with a laugh.

It was broad daylight. I sat up and looked around. 'We have survived another night,' I said.

'And face another day of – what?' she demanded.

'Who knows?'

I gathered some fruit, and we cooked some more of the meat left from my kill of the previous day. We had a splendid breakfast, and then we set off again down stream in our quest for – what?

'If we do not find Duare today,' I said, 'I shall have to admit that she is irrevocably lost to me.'

'And then what?, asked Nalte.

'You would like to return to your own country?'

'Of course,'

'Then we shall start up the big river toward your home.'

'We shall never reach it,' said Nalte, 'but ——'

'But what?' I demanded.

'I was thinking that we might be very happy while we were trying to reach Andoo,' she said.

'Andoo?' I queried.

'That is my country,' she explained. 'The mountains of Andoo are very beautiful.'

There was a note of wistfulness in her voice; her eyes were contemplating a scene that mine could not see. Suddenly I realized how brave the girl had been, how cheerful she had remained through the hardships and menacing dangers of our flight, all despite the probable hopelessness of her situation. I touched her hand gently.

'We shall do our best to return you to the beautiful mountains of Andoo,' I assured her.

Nalte shook her head. 'I shall never see them again, Carson. A great company of warriors might not survive the dangers that lie bewteen here and Andoo – a thousand kobs of fierce and hostile country – so how could you and I hope to succeed alone?'

'A thousand kobs is a long way,' I agreed. 'It does seem hopeless, but we'll not give up.'

The Amtorians divide the circumference of a circle into a thousand parts to arrive at their hita, or degree; and the kob is one tenth of a degree of longitude at the equator (or what the Amtorians call The Small Circle), roughly about 2½ earth miles; therefore a thousand kobs would be about 2500 miles.

A little mental arithmetic convinced me that Nalte could not have drifted down the big river 2500 miles without food, and I asked her if she were sure that Andoo was that far away.

'No,' she admitted, 'but is seems that far. We wandered a long time before we reached the river, and then I drifted for so long that I lost track of time.'

Nevertheless, if we found Duare, I was going to be faced by a problem. One girl must go down the valley in search of her own country, the other up the valley! And only one of them had even a hazy idea of where her country lay!

CHAPTER 10

THE LAST SECOND

DURING the afternoon of the second day of our search for Duare, Nalte and I came to the big river that Duare and I had seen from the summit of the escarpment, the same river down which Nalte had drifted into the clutches of Skor.

And it was a big river, comparable to the Mississippi. It ran between low cliffs of gleaming white limestone, flowing silently out of the mystery above, flowing silently toward the mystery below. Upon its broad expanse, from where it swept majestically into sight around a low promontory to where it disappeared again beyond a curve down stream, there was no sign of life, nor on either bank – only the girl, Nalte, and I. I felt the awe of its grandeur and my own insignificance.

I had no words to express my thoughts; and I was glad that Nalte stood in silence, that was almost reverential, as we viewed the majesty and the desolation of the scene.

Presently the girl sighed. It awoke me to the needs of the moment. I could not stand mooning there in the face of the immediate necessity that confronted us.

'Well,' I said, 'this is not crossing the river.' I referred to the affluent that we had followed down from the castle of Skor.

'I am glad that we do not have to cross the big river,' remarked Nalte.

'We may have enough trouble crossing this other,' I suggested.

It flowed at our left, making a sudden turn before it emptied into the larger stream. Below us was a great eddy that had strewn the nearer bank with flotsam – leaves, twigs, branches of all sizes, and even the boles of great trees. These things appeared to have been deposited during a period of high water.

'How are we going to cross?' asked Nalte. 'There is no ford, and it seems too wide and swift to swim even if I were a good swimmer.' She looked up at me quickly then as a new thought seemed to strike her. 'I am a burden to you,' she said. 'If you were alone, you would doubtless be able to cross easily. Pay no attention to me; I shall remain on this side and start up the river on my journey toward Andoo, while you cross and search for Duare.'

I looked down at her and smiled. 'You really do not believe nor hope that I will do anything of the sort.'

'It would be the sensible thing to do,' she said.

'The sensible thing to do is to build a raft with some of that stuff down there and float across the river.' I pointed to the debris piled up on the bank.

'Why, we could do that, couldn't we?' she cried.

She was all eagerness and excitement now, and a moment later she pitched in and helped me drag out such pieces as I thought we could use in the construction of a raft.

It was hard work, but at last we had enough material to float us in safety. The next job was to fasten the elements of our prospective raft together so securely that the river could not tear it to pieces before we had gained the opposite bank.

We gathered lianas for that purpose, and though we worked as rapidly as we could it was almost dark before we had completed our rude ferry.

As I contemplated the fruit of our labor, I saw Nalte surveying the swirling waters of the eddy with a dubious eye.

'Are we going to cross now,' she asked, 'or wait until morning?'

'It is almost dark now,' I replied; 'I think we had better wait until tomorrow.'

She brightened visibly and drew a deep sigh of relief. 'Then we had better think about eating now,' she said. I had found the girls of Venus not unlike their earthly sisters in this respect.

The meal that night was a matter of fruit and tubers, but it was sufficient. Once more I constructed a platform among the branches of a tree, and prayed that no prowling arboreal carnivore would discover us.

Each morning that I awoke on Venus it was with a sense of surprise that I still lived, and this first morning on the big river was no exception.

As soon as we had eaten we went to our raft, and after some difficulty succeeded in launching it. I had equipped it with several long branches for poling and some short ones that we might use as oars after we got into the deep channel, but they were most inadequate makeshifts. I was depending almost exclusively on the eddy to carry us within striking distance of the opposite shore, where I hoped that we would then be able to pole the raft to the bank.

Our craft floated much better than I had anticipated. I had feared that it would be almost awash and most uncomfortable; but the wood was evidently light, with the result that the top of the raft was several inches above the water.

No sooner had we shoved off than the eddy seized us and commenced to bear us up stream and out toward the center. Our only concern now was to keep from being drawn into the vortex, and by poling frantically we managed to keep near the periphery of the whirlpool until the water deepened to such a degree that our poles would no longer touch bottom; then we seized the shorter branches and rowed desperately. It was gruelling work, yet Nalte never faltered.

At last we swung in toward the left bank; and once more we seized our poles, but to my astonishment and chagrin I discovered that the water here was still too deep. The current, too, was much stronger on this side on than the other; and our futile oars were almost useless.

Remorselessly the river held us in its grip and dragged us back toward the vortex. We paddled furiously and held our own; we were keeping away from the center of the eddy, but we were being carried farther from the left bank.

Presently we were in mid-channel. We seemed to be hanging on the very edge of the eddy. Both of us were almost exhausted by this time, yet we might not pause for an instant. With a last, supreme effort we tore the raft from the clutches of the current that would have drawn us back into the embrace of the swirling Titan; then the main current of the mid-channel seized us – a fierce, relentless force. Our craft swirled and bobbed about absolutely beyond control, and we were swept down toward the great river.

I laid aside my inadequate paddle. 'We have done our best, Nalte,' I said, 'but it wasn't good enough. Now all that we can do is to hope that this thing will hang together until we drift to one shore or the other somewhere along the big river.'

'It will have to be soon,' said Nalte.

'Why?' I asked.

'When Skor found me, he said that I was fortunate to have come to shore where I did, as farther down the river tumbles over falls.'

I looked at the low cliffs that lined the river on both sides. 'There isn't any chance of making a landing here,' I said.

'Perhaps we shall have better luck lower down,' suggested Nalte.

Down we drifted with the current, sometimes borne close to one shore, sometimes close to the other as the channel meandered from bank to bank; or again we rode far out on the center of the flood. Sometimes we saw little breaks in the cliffs where we might have made a landing; but we always saw them too late, and were carried past before we could maneuver our clumsy craft within reach.

As we approached each bend, we looked expectantly for some change in the shore line that would offer us some hope of landing, but always we were disappointed. And then, at last, as we swung around a headland, we saw two cities. One lay upon the left bank of the river, the other on the right directly opposite. The former appeared grey and drab even at a distance, while that upon the right bank shone white and beautiful and gay with its limestone walls and towers and its roofs of many colors.

Nalte nodded toward the city on the left bank. 'That must be Kormor; this is about the location that Skor told me his city occupied.'

'And the other? What is that?' I asked.

She shook her head. 'Skor never mentioned another city.'

'Perhaps it is all one city built upon both banks of the river,' I suggested.

'No; I do not think so. Skor told me that the people who dwelt across the river from Kormor were his enemies, but he never said anything about a city. I thought it was just some savage tribe. Why, that is a splendid city – far larger and handsomer than Kormor.'

We could not, of course, see the entire expanse of either city; but as we drifted closer it was apparent that the city on our right extended along the river front for several miles. This we could see because at this point the river ran almost as straight as a canal for a greater distance than I could see. But the city on our left, which was Kormor, was much smaller, extending but about a mile along the water front.

As far as we could see both cities were walled, a high wall extending along the river side of each. Kormor had a short quay in front of a gate about the center of this wall, while the quay of the other city appeared to be a long avenue extending as far as I could see.

We had been drifting for some time opposite the right hand city before we came close to Kormor. There were a few fishermen on the long quay of the former city and others, possibly sentries, on top of the wall behind them. Many of these saw us and pointed at us and seemed to be discussing us, but at no time did we drift close enough to that side of the river so that we could obtain a close view of them or hail them.

As we came down toward the quay of Kormor, a small boat pushed out into the river. It contained three men, two of whom were rowing while the third stood in the bow. That they were pulling out to intercept us appeared quite evident.

'They are Skor's men,' said Nalte, with a shudder.

'What do you suppose they want of us?' I asked.

'To capture us, of course, for Skor; but they will never capture me!' She stepped toward the edge of the raft.

'What do you mean?' I demanded. 'What are you going to do?'

'I am going to jump into the river.'

'But you can't swim,' I objected. 'You will be sure to drown.'

'That is what I wish to do. I shall never let Skor take me again.'

'Wait, Nalte,' I begged. 'They haven't taken us yet. Perhaps they won't.'

'Yes, they will,' she said hopelessly.

'We must never give up hope, Nalte. Promise me that you will wait. Even in the last second you can still carry out your plan.'

'I will wait,' she promised, 'but in the last second you had better follow my example and join me in death rather than fall into the hands of Skor and become one of those hopeless creatures that you saw at his castle, for then you will be denied even the final escape of death.'

The boat was now approaching closer, and I hailed its occupants. 'What do you want of us?' I demanded.

'You must come ashore with us,' said the man in the bow.

I was close enough now so that I could get a good look at the fellow. I had thought at first that they were some more of Skor's living dead, but now I saw that this fellow's cheeks had the hue of health and blood.

'We will not come with you,' I called back to him. 'Leave us alone; we are not harming you. Let us go on our way in peace.'

'You will come ashore with us,' said the man, as his boat drew closer.

'Keep away, or I'll kill you!' I cried, fitting an arrow to my bow.

The fellow laughed – a dry, mirthless laugh. Then it was that I saw his eyes, and a cold chill swept over me. They were the dead eyes of a corpse!

I loosed an arrow. It drove straight through the creature's chest, but it only laughed again and left the arrow sticking there.

'Do you not know,' cried Nalte, 'that you cannot kill the dead?' She stepped to the far side of the raft. 'Good-bye, Carson,' she said quietly; 'the last second is here!'

'No! No, Nalte!' I cried. 'Wait! It is not the last second.'

I turned again toward the approaching boat. Its bow was already within a foot of the raft. Before the fellow standing in it could grasp my intention I leaped upon him. He struck at me with his dead hands; his dead fingers clutched for my throat. But my attack had been too quick and unexpected. I had carried him off his balance, and in the same instant I seized him and threw him overboard.

The two other creatures had been rowing with their backs toward the bow and were unaware that any danger threatened them until I crashed upon their leader. As he went overboard, the nearer of the others rose and turned upon me. His skin, too, was painted in the semblance of life, but those dead eyes could not be changed.

With a horrid, inarticulate scream he leaped for me. I met his rush with a right to the jaw that would have knocked a living man down for a long count; and while, of course, I couldn't knock the thing out, I did knock it overboard.

A quick glance at the two in the water convinced me that my guess had not been amiss – like their fellows at the castle, the two could not swim and were floating helplessly down stream with the current. But there was still another, and it was stepping across the thwarts toward me.

I sprang forward to meet it, ripping in a blow toward the side of the jaw that would have sent it after the other two had it connected; but it did not. Our movements caused the boat to rock and threw me off my balance, and before I could regain my equilibrium the creature seized me.

It was very powerful, but it fought without fire or enthusiasm – just the cold, deadly application of force. It reached for my throat; to reach for its were useless. I could not choke the life from something that had no life. The best that I could do was to try to evade its clutches and wait for an opening that might never come.

I am rather muscular myself; and I did manage to push the thing from me for a moment, but it came right back. It didn't say anything; it didn't make any sound at all. There was no expression in its glazed eyes, but its dry lips were drawn back over yellow teeth in a snarling grimace. The sight of it and the touch of those cold, clammy fingers almost unnerved me – these and the strange odor that emanated from it, the strange odor that is the odor of death. It was sickening.

As it came toward me the second time it came with lowered head and outstretched arms. I leaped for it, and locked my right arm about its head from above. The back of its neck was snug against my armpit as I seized my own right wrist with my left hand and locked my hold tighter. Then I swung quickly around, straightening up as I did so and, incidentally, nearly capsizing the boat. The creature lost its footing as I swung it about; its arms flailed wildly, as with a last mighty surge I released my hold and sent it stumbling over the gunwale into the river. Like the others, it floated away, apparently helpless.

A few yards away, the raft was drifting with Nalte wide-eyed and tense with excitement. Seizing an oar I brought the boat alongside and, extending a hand, assisted Nalte over the side. I noticed that she was trembling.

'Frightened?' I asked.

'For you, yes. I didn't think that you had a chance against three of them. Even now I can't believe what I saw. It is incredible that one man could have done what you did.'

'Luck had a lot to do with it,' I replied, 'and the fact that

I took them by surprise. They weren't expecting anything of the sort.'

'How strangely things happen,' mused Nalte. 'A moment ago I was about to drown myself in sheer desperation, and now everything is changed. The danger is over, and instead of an inadequate raft we have a comfortable boat.'

'Which proves that one should never give up hope.'

'I shan't again – while you are with me,' she promised.

I had been keeping an eye on the Kormor quay rather expecting to see another boat put out in pursuit of us, but none did. The fishermen and the sentries on the water front of the other city had all stopped what they were doing and were watching us.

'Shall we row over there and see if they will take us in?' I asked.

'I am afraid,' replied Nalte. 'We have a saying in Andoo that the farther strangers are away the better friends they are.'

'You think that they would harm us?' I asked.

Nalte shrugged. 'I do not know, but the chances are that they would kill you and keep me.'

'Then we won't take the chance, but I would like to remain near here for a while and search for Duare.'

'You can't land on the left bank until we are out of sight of Kormor,' said Nalte, 'or they would be after us in no time.'

'And if we land in sight of this other city, these people would take after us, if what you fear be true.'

'Let's go down stream until we are out of sight of both cities,' suggested the girl, 'and then wait until night before coming back near Kormor to search, for that is where you will have to search for Duare.'

Following Nalte's suggestion we drifted slowly down stream. We soon passed Kormor, but the white city on the right bank extended on for a couple of miles further. I should say that its full length along the river front was fully five miles, and along all that length was the broad quay backed by a gleaming white wall pierced by an occasional gate – I counted six or seven along the full length of the water front.

Just below the city the river turned to the right, and almost immediately the cliffs shut off our view of both cities.

Simultaneously the aspect of the country changed. The limestone cliffs ended abruptly, the river running between low banks. Here it spread out to considerable width, but farther ahead I could see where it narrowed again and entered a gorge between cliffs much higher than any that we had passed. They were wooded cliffs, and even from a distance I could see that they were not of the white limestone that formed those with which we had now become familiar.

There came to my ears faintly an insistent sound that was at first little more than a murmur, but as we drifted down the river it seemed to grow constantly in volume.

'Do you hear what I hear?' I demanded, 'or am I the victim of head noises?'

'That distant roaring?'

'Yes; it has become a roar now. What do you suppose it can be?'

'It must be the falls that Skor told me of,' said Nalte.

'By Jove! that's just what it is,' I exclaimed. 'And the best thing we can do is to get to shore while we can.'

The current had carried us closer to the right bank at this point, and just ahead of us I saw a small stream emptying into the river. There was an open forest on the farther side of the stream and scattered trees on the nearer. It appeared an ideal location for a camp.

We made the shore easily, for the current here was not swift. I ran the boat into the mouth of the small stream, but there was not water enough to float it. However, I managed to drag it up far enough to tie it to an overhanging limb of a tree where it was out of sight of any possible pursuers from Kormor who might come down the river in search of us.

'Now,' I said, 'the thing that interests me most at present is food.'

'That is something that always interests me,' admitted Nalte, with a laugh. 'Where are you going to hunt? That forest on the other side of this little stream looks as though it should be filled with game.'

She was facing the forest as she spoke, while my back was toward it. Suddenly the expression on her face changed, and she seized my arm with a little cry of alarm. 'Look Carson! What is that?'

CHAPTER 11

To Live or Die?

As I turned at Nalte's warning cry, I thought that I saw something dodge behind low bushes on the opposite bank.

'What was it, Nalte? Did you see what it was?' I demanded.

'Oh, it couldn't be what I thought I saw,' she whispered excitedly. 'I must be mistaken.'

'What did you think you saw?'

'There's another – there – look!' she cried.

And then I saw it. It stepped from behind the bole of a large trees and stood eyeing us, its fangs bared in a snarl. It was a man that went on four feet like a beast. Its hind legs were short, and it walked on its hind toes, the heels corresponding with the hocks of animals. Its hands were more human, and it walked flat on the palms of them in front. Its nose was flat, its mouth broad, and its heavy, undershot jaws were armed with powerful teeth. Its eyes were small and close set and extremely savage. Its skin was white and almost hairless except upon its head and jowls.

'You don't know what they are?' I asked Nalte.

'We have heard of them in Andoo, but no one ever believed that they existed. They are called zangans. If the stories I have heard are true, they are terribly ferocious. They hunt in packs and devour men as well as beasts.'

Zangan means beast-man, and no better word could have been coined to describe the creature that faced us across that little stream in far Noobol. And now others came slinking in to view from the shelter of bushes and from behind the boles of trees.

'I think we had better hunt elsewhere,' I said in a sickly effort to be jocose.

'Let's take to the boat again,' suggested Nalte.

We had already walked a little distance from the spot where I had moored our craft, and as we turned to retrace our steps I saw several of the zangans enter the water on the opposite side and approach the boat. They were much closer to it than we, and long before I could untie it and drag it into deeper water they could be upon us.

'It is too late,' cried Nalte.

'Let's fall back slowly to that little rise of ground behind us,' I said. 'Perhaps I can hold them off there.'

We retreated slowly, watching the zangans as they crossed the stream toward us. When they came out on shore, they shook themselves as dogs do, and then they came slinking after us again. They reminded me of tigers – human tigers – and their gait was much that of a stalking tiger as they approached with flattened heads and snarling lips.

They growled and snapped at one another, revealing a viciousness greater than that of beasts. Momentarily I expected a charge, and I knew that when it came Nalte's troubles and mine would be over forever. We wouldn't have even a fighting chance against that savage pack.

There were about twenty of them, mostly males; but there were a couple of females and two or three half-grown cubs. On the back of one of the females rode a baby, its arms tightly hugging the neck of its mother.

Savage as they appeared, they followed us warily as though they were half afraid of us; but their long, easy strides were constantly cutting down the distance between us.

When we reached the little mound toward which we had been retreating, they were still fifty yards behind us. As we started to ascend the rise, a large male trotted forward, voicing a low roar. It was as though it had just occurred to him that we might be trying to escape and that he ought to try to prevent it.

I stopped and faced him, fitting an arrow to my bow. Drawing the shaft back to the very tip I let him have it squarely in the chest. He stopped in his tracks, roared horribly, and clawed at the feathered end protruding from his body; then he came on again; but he was staggering, and presently he sank to the ground, struggled for a moment, and lay still.

The others had stopped and were watching him. Suddenly a young male ran up to him and bit him savagely about the head and neck; then raised his head and voiced a hideous roar. I guessed that it was a challenge as I saw him look about him at the other members of the pack. Here, perhaps, was a new leader usurping the powers of him who had fallen.

Apparently no one was prepared to question his authority, and now he turned his attention again to us. He did not advance directly toward us, but slunk off to one side. As he did so he turned and growled at his fellows. That he was communicating orders to them at once became evident, for immediately they spread out as though to surround us.

I loosed another arrow then, this time at the new leader. It struck him in the side just forward of the stifle, and elicited such a roar of pain and rage as I hope I may never hear again – at least not under such circumstances.

Reaching back with one hand the beast-man seized the shaft and tore it from his body, inflicting a far more serious hurt than the arrow had made in entering; and now his roars and screams fairly shook the ground.

The others paused to watch him, and I saw one large male slink slowly toward the wounded leader. The latter saw him, too; and with bared fangs and ferocious growls charged him. The ambitious one, evidently realizing that his hopes had been premature, wheeled and fled; and the new chief let him go and turned again toward us.

By this time we were three-quarters surrounded. There were nearly twenty ferocious beasts confronting us, and I had less than a dozen arrows.

Nalte touched me on the arm. 'Good-bye, Carson,' she said; 'now, surely, the last second is upon us.'

I shook my head. 'I am saving the last second in which to die,' I replied. 'Until then I shall not admit that there is ever to be a last second for me, and then it will be too late to matter.'

'I admire your courage if not your reasoning,' said Nalte, the ghost of a smile touching her lips. 'But at least it will be a quick death – did you see how that fellow tore at the throat of the first one you shot? It is better than what Skor would have done to us.'

'At least we shall be dead,' I observed.

'Here they come!' cried Nalte.

They were closing in on us now from three sides. Arrow after arrow I drove into them, nor once did I miss my mark; but they only stopped those that I hit – the others came on.

They were almost upon us as I loosed my last arrow. Nalte was standing close beside me. I put an arm about her.

'Hold me close,' she said. 'I am not afraid to die, but I do not want to be alone – even for an instant.'

'You are not dead yet, Nalte.' I couldn't think of anything else to say. It must have sounded foolish at such a time, but Nalte ignored it.

'You have been very good to me, Carson,' she said.

'And you have been a regular brick, Nalte, if you know what that means – which you don't.'

'Good-bye, Carson? It *is* the last second.'

'I guess it is, Nalte.' I stooped and kissed her. 'Good-bye!'

From above us and behind us on the mound came a sudden cracking hum that was like the noise that an X-ray machine makes, but I knew that it was not an X-ray machine. I knew what it was even without the evidence of the crumpling bodies of the sangans dropping to the ground before us – it was the hum of the r-ray rifle of Amtor!

I wheeled and looked up toward the summit of the mound. There stood a dozen men pouring streams of the destructive rays upon the pack. It lasted for but a few seconds, but not one of the ferocious beasts escaped death. Then one of our rescuers (or were they our captors) came toward us.

He, like his companions, was a man of almost perfect physique with a handsome, intelligent face. My first impression was that if these were fair examples of the citizens of that white city from which I assumed they had come, we must have stumbled upon an Olympus inhabited solely by gods.

In every company of men we are accustomed to seeing some whose proportions or features are ungainly or uncouth; but these all were singularly handsome and symmetrically proportioned.

He who approached us wore the customary G string and military harness of the men of Amtor. His trappings were handsome without being ornate, and I guessed from the insignia on the fillet that encircled his brow that he was an officer.

'You had a close call,' he said pleasantly.

'Rather too close for comfort,' I replied. 'We have you to thank for our lives.'

'I am glad that I arrived in time. I happened to be on the river wall as you drifted past, and saw your encounter with the men from Kormor. My interest was aroused; and, knowing that you were headed for trouble down river on account of the falls, I gathered some of my men and hurried down to try to warn you.'

'A rather unusual interest in strangers for a man of Amtor,' I said, 'but I assure you that I appreciate it even if I do not understand it.'

He laughed shortly. 'It was the way you handled those three creatures of Skor,' he explained. 'I saw possibilities in such a man, and we are always looking for better qualities to infuse into the blood of Havatoo. But come, let me introduce myself. I am Ero Shan,'

'And this is Nalte of Andoo,' I replied, 'and I am Carson Napier of California.'

'I have heard of Andoo,' he acknowledged. 'They raise an exceptionally fine breed of people there, but I never heard of your country. In fact I have never seen a man before with blue eyes and yellow hair. Are all the people of Cal ——'

'California,' I prompted.

'— of California like you?'

'Oh, no! There are all colors among us, of hair and eyes and skin.'

'But how can you breed true to type then?' he demanded.

'We don't,' I had to admit.

'Rather shocking,' he said, half to himself, 'immoral – racially immoral. Well, be that as it may, your system seems to have produced a rather fine type at that; and now, if you will come with me, we shall return to Havatoo.'

'May I ask,' I inquired, 'if we return as guests or prisoners?'

He smiled, just the shadow of a smile. 'Will that make any difference – as to whether you return with me or not?'

I glanced up at the armed men behind him and grinned. 'None,' I replied.

'Let us be friends,' he said. 'You will find in Havatoo, justice. If you deserve to remain as a guest, you will be treated as a guest – if not –' he shrugged.

As we reached the top of the little hillock we saw, just behind it, a long, low car with transverse seats and no top. The severity of its stream lines and its lack of ornamentation suggested that it was a military car.

As we entered the rear seat with Ero Shan his men took their places in the forward seats. Ero Shan spoke a word of command, and the car moved forward. The driver was too far from me and hidden by the men between us to permit me to see how he controlled the car, which moved forward over the uneven ground smoothly and swiftly.

Presently as we topped a rise of ground we saw the city of Havatoo lying white and beautiful before us. From our elevation I could see that it was built in the shape of a half circle with the flat side lying along the water front, and it was entirely walled.

The river curves to the right below the city, and the direct route that we followed returning to it brought us to a gate several miles from the river. The gate itself was of magnificent proportions and an architectural gem, bespeaking a high order of civilization and culture. The city wall, of white limestone, was beautifully carved with scenes that I took to portray the history of the city or of the race that inhabited it, the work having apparently been conceived and executed with the rarest taste; and these carvings extended as far as I could see.

When one considers the fact that the wall is fully thirteen miles long and that all of it is elaborately carved, one may understand the vast labor and the time required to complete such an undertaking along both faces of a twenty-foot wall.

As we were halted at the gate by the soldiers on guard, I saw emblazoned above the portal in the characters of the universal Amtorian language, *Tag Kum Voo Klambad*, Gate of the Psychologists.

Beyond the gate we entered a broad, straight avenue that ran directly toward the center of the water front. It was filled with traffic – cars of various sizes and shapes, running swiftly and quietly in both directions. There was nothing but vehicular traffic on this level, pedestrians being accommodated on walkways at the level of the second stories of the buildings, which were connected by viaducts at all intersections.

There was practically no noise – no tooting of horns, no screeching of brakes – traffic regulated itself. I asked Ero Shan about it.

'It is very simple,' he said. 'All vehicles are energized from a central power station from which power emanates in three frequencies; on the control board of each vehicle is a dial that permits the operator to pick up any frequency that he desires. One is for avenues running from the outer wall to the center of the city, another is for transverse avenues, and the third for all traffic outside the city. The first two are cut off and on alternately; when one is on, all traffic moving in the opposite direction is stopped at intersections automatically.'

'But why doesn't the traffic between intersections stop at the same time?' I asked.

'That is regulated by the third frequency which is always operative,' he explained. 'A hundred feet before a vehicle reaches an inter-section a photo-electric current moves the dial on the control board to the proper frequency for that lane.'

Nalte was thrilled by all that she saw. She was a mountain girl from a small kingdom, and this was the first large city that she had ever seen.

'It is marvellous,' she said. 'And how beautiful the people are!'

I had noticed that fact myself. Both the men and the women in the cars that passed us were of extraordinary perfection of form and feature.

Ambad Lat, Psychologist Avenue, led us directly to a semicircular civic center at the water front from which the principal avenues radiated toward the outer wall like the spokes of a wheel from the hub toward the felloe.

Here were magnificent buildings set in a gorgeous park, and here Ero Shan escorted us from the car toward a splendid palace. There were many people in the park, going to or coming from the various buildings. There was no hurry, no bustle, no confusion; nor was there idling nor loitering. All suggested well considered, unhurried efficiency. The voices of those who conversed were pleasant, well modulated. Like the people I had seen elsewhere in the city, these were all handsome and well formed.

We followed Ero Shan through an entrance into a wide

corridor. Many of those we passed spoke pleasant greetings to our companion, and all of them looked at us with seemingly friendly interest but without rudeness.

'Beautiful people in a beautiful city,' murmured Nalte.

Ero Shan turned toward her with a quick smile. 'I am glad that you like us and Havatoo,' he said. 'I hope that nothing will ever alter this first impression.'

'You think that something may?' asked Nalte.

Ero Shan shrugged. 'That all depends upon you,' he replied, 'or rather upon your ancestors.'

'I do not understand,' said Nalte.

'You will presently.'

He stopped before a door and swinging it open bade us enter. We were in a small ante-room in which several clerks were employed.

'Please inform Korgan Kantum Mohar that I wish to see him,' said Ero Shan to one of the clerks.

The man pressed one of several buttons on his desk and said, 'Korgan Sentar Ero Shan wishes to see you.'

Apparently from the desk top a deep voice replied, 'Send him in.'

'Come with me,' directed Ero Shan, and we crossed the anteroom to another door which a clerk arose and opened. In the room beyond a man faced us from a desk behind which he was seated. He looked up at us with the same friendly interest that had been manifested by the people we had passed in the park and the corridor.

As we were introduced to Korgan Kantum Mohar he arose and acknowledged the introduction with a bow; then he invited us to be seated.

'You are strangers in Havatoo,' he remarked. 'It is not often that strangers enter our gates.' He turned to Ero Shan. 'How did it happen?'

Ero Shan told of witnessing my encounter with the three men from Kormor. 'I hated to see a man like this go over the falls,' he continued, 'and I felt that it was worth while bringing them into Havatoo for an examination. Therefore I have brought them directly to you, hoping that you will agree with me.'

'It can do no harm,' admitted Mohar. 'The examining board is in session now. Take them over. I will advise the board that I have authorized the examination.'

'What is the examination, and what is its purpose?' I asked. 'Perhaps we do not care to take it.'

Korgan Kantum Mohar smiled. 'It is not for you to say,' he said.

'You mean that we are prisoners?'

'Let us say rather guests by command.'

'Do you mind telling me the purpose of this examination?' I asked.

'Not at all. It is to determine whether or not you shall be permitted to live.'

CHAPTER 12

Havatoo

They were all very polite and pleasant, very professional and efficient. First we were bathed; then blood tests were made, our hearts examined, our blood pressure taken, our reflexes checked. After that we were ushered into a large room where five men sat behind a long table.

Ero Shan accompanied us throughout the examination. Like the others, he was always pleasant and friendly. He encouraged us to hope that we would pass the examination successfully. Even yet I did not understand what it was all about. I asked Ero Shan.

'Your companion remarked upon the beauty of Havatoo and its people,' he replied. 'This examination is the explanation of that beauty – and of many other things here which you do not yet know of.'

The five men seated behind the long table were quite as pleasant as any of the others we had met. They questioned us rapidly for fully an hour and then they dismissed us. From the questions propounded I judged that one of them was a biologist, another a psychologist, one a chemist, the fourth a physicist, and the fifth a soldier.

'Korgan Sentar Ero Shan,' said he who appeared to be the head of the examining board, 'you will take custody of the man until the result of the examination is announced. Hara Es will take charge of the girl.' He indicated a woman who had entered the room with us and had been standing beside Nalte.

The latter pressed closer to me. 'Oh, Carson! They are going to separate us,' she whispered.

I turned toward Ero Shan to expostulate, but he motioned me to be silent. 'You will have to obey,' he said, 'but I think you have no reason to worry.'

Then Nalte was led away by Hara Es, and Ero Shan took me with him. A car was waiting for Ero Shan, and in it we were driven into a district of beautiful homes. Presently the car drew up in front of one of these and stopped.

'This is my home,' said my companion. 'You will be my

guest here until the result of the examination is announced. I wish you to enjoy yourself while you are with me. Do not worry; it will do no good. Nalte is safe. She will be well cared for.'

'At least they have provided me with a beautiful prison and a pleasant jailer,' I remarked.

'Please do not think of yourself as a prisoner,' begged Ero Shan. 'It will make us both unhappy, and unhappiness is not to be tolerated in Havatoo.'

'I am far from unhappy,' I assured him. 'On the contrary I am greatly enjoying the experience, but I still cannot understand what crime is charged against Nalte and me that we should have been put on trial for our lives."

'It was not you who were on trial, it was your heredity,' he explained.

'An explanation,' I assured him, 'that leaves me as much at sea as I was before.'

We had entered the house as we were conversing, and I found myself amid as lovely surroundings as I have ever seen. Good taste and good judgment had evidently dictated, not only the design of the house but its appointments as well. From the entrance there was a vista of shrubbery and flowers and trees in a beautiful garden at the end of a wide hall. It was to this garden that Ero Shan led me and then to an apartment that opened upon it.

'You will find everything here for your convenience and comfort,' he said. 'I shall detail a man to wait upon you; he will be courteous and efficient. But he will also be responsible for your presence when it is again required at the Central Laboratories.

'And now,' he said, seating himself in a chair near a window, 'let me try to answer your last question more explicitly.

'Havatoo and the race that inhabits it are the result of generations of scientific culture. Originally we were a people ruled by hereditary jongs that various factions sought to dominate for their own enrichment and without consideration for the welfare of the remainder of the people.

'If we had a good jong who was also a strong character, we were well ruled; otherwise the politicians misruled us. These politicians were opportunists, demagogues, or worse. For the most part they were men without culture or great intelligence, for the better classes would not enter politics where they were forced to mingle with men of this stamp.

'Half of our people lived in direst poverty, in vice, in filth; and they bred like flies. The better classes, refusing to bring children into such a world, dwindled rapidly. Ignorance and mediocrity ruled.

'Then a great jong came to the throne. He abrogated all existing laws and government and vested both in himself. Two titles have been conferred upon him – one while he lived, the other after his death. The first was Mankar the Bloody; the second, Mankar the Saviour.

'He was a great warrior, and he had the warrior class behind him. With what seemed utter ruthlessness he wiped out the politicians, and to the positions many of them had filled he appointed the greatest minds of Havatoo – physicists, biologists, chemists, and psychologists.

'He encouraged the raising of children by people whom these scientists passed as fit to raise children, and he forbade all others to bear children. He saw to it that the physically, morally, or mentally defective were rendered incapable of bringing their like into the world; and no defective infant was allowed to live.

'Then, before his death, he created a new form of government – a government without laws and without a king. He abdicated his throne and relinquished the destinies of Havatoo to a quintumvirate that but guides and judges.

'Of these five men one is a sentar (biologist), one an ambad (psychologist), one a kalto (chemist), one a kantum (physicist), and one a korgan (soldier). This quintumvirate is called Sanjong (literally, five-king), and the fitness of its members to serve is determined by examinations similar to that which was given you. These examinations are held every two years. Any citizen may take them; any citizen may become one of the Sanjong. It is the highest honor to which a citizen of Havatoo may win, and he may only achieve it through actual merit. His qualifications are not left to the guesswork of an electorate influenced by the heat and passion and misrepresentations of a political campaign, or to an accident of birth that made one man a slave and another a king.'

'And these men make the laws and administer justice,' I remarked.

'There are no laws in Havatoo,' replied Ero Shan. 'During the many generations since Mankar we have bred a race of rational people who know the difference between right and wrong, and for such no rules of behaviour are necessary. The Sanjong merely guides. When new problems arise that are beyond the experience of our people, the Sanjong states what it believes to be the proper course of action. If a citizen fails to follow the suggestions of the Sanjong, and harm results, the citizen is then brought to judgment.

'Of course we are not perfect; no man may ever be, but wilful actions that are harmful to our fellows or to Havatoo are extremely rare.'

'Do you have any difficulty in finding the proper men to form the Sanjong?' I asked.

'None whatever. There are thousands of men in Havatoo capable of serving with honor and distinction. There is a tendency to breed Sanjongs among five of the six classes into which the people of Havatoo are naturally divided.

'When you become more familiar with the city, you will discover that the semicircular area facing the Central Laboratories is divided into five sections. The section next to the river and above the Central Laboratories is called Kantum. Here reside the physicists. There are no caste distinctions between the physicists and any of the other five classes, but because they all live in the same district and because their interests are alike, there is a greater tendency for them to associate with one another than with members of other classes. The result is that they more often mate with their own kind – the laws of heredity do the rest, and the breed of physicists in Havatoo is constantly improving, with the result that we constantly find a better physicist winning a place on the Sanjong as the years go by.

'The next district is Kalto; here live the chemists. The center district is Korgan, the district in which I dwell. It is reserved for the warrior class. Next comes Ambad, the section where the psychologists live; and, last, Sentar, for the biologists, lies along the water front below the Central Laboratories.

'Havatoo is laid out like the half of a wagon wheel with the Central Laboratories at the hub. The main sections of the city are bounded by four concentric semicircles. Inside the first is the civic center where the Central Laboratories are situated; this I have called the hub. Between this and the next semicircle lie the five sub-districts I have just described. Between this and the third semicircle lies the largest district, called Yorgan; here dwell the common people. And in the fourth section, a narrow strip just inside the outer wall, are the shops, markets, and factories.'

'It is all most interesting,' I said, 'and to me the most interesting part of it is that the city is governed without laws.'

'Without man-made laws,' Ero Shan corrected me. 'We are governed by natural laws with which all intelligent people are conversant; by applying eugenics intelligently we have eliminated the unintelligent.

'Of course occasionally a citizen commits an act that is harmful to another or to the peace of the city, for the genes of vicious and nonconformist characteristics have not all been eradicated from the germ cells of all of the citizens of Havatoo.

'If one commits an act that is subversive of the rights of others or of the general welfare of the community, he is tried by a court that is not hampered by technicalities nor precedent and which, taking into consideration all of the facts in the case, including the heredity of the defendant, reaches a decision that is final and without appeal.

'The result of the act itself is never considered; our courts seek causes only. There is no punishment in the sense that it was formerly understood. The sole aim of the courts is to prevent a repetition of unsocial acts by this and future generations.

'If it is a first offense in four generations of the defendant's family, it is merely recorded against his blood line. For the second offense of a minor nature he is placed under observation. For more serious infractions or for a repetition of minor ones he is rendered incapable of perpetuating his type; and, as a rule, for any fourth offense he is destroyed.'

'It seems rather drastic to punish a man for the acts of his ancestors,' I remarked.

'But let me remind you that we do not punish,' explained Ero Shan; 'we only seek to improve the race to the end that we shall attain the greatest measures of happiness and contentment. Nonconformists are not good material with which to improve a race nor are people who make too many mistakes.'

'Havatoo, with no bad people in it, must be an ideal city in which to live,' I said.

'Oh, there are some bad people,' replied Ero Shan, 'for there are bad genes in all of us; but we are a very intelligent race, and the more intelligent people are, the better able are they to control their bad impulses. Occasionally strangers enter Havatoo, bad men from the city across the river. How they accomplish it is a mystery that has never been solved, but we know that they come and steal a man or a woman occasionally. Sometimes we catch them, and when we do we destroy them. Rarely, our own people commit crimes, usually crimes of passion; but occasionally one commits a premeditated crime. The latter are a menace to the race and are not permitted to survive and transmit their characteristics to future generations or influence the present by their bad examples.'

As he ceased speaking a very powerfully built man came to the door of the room. 'You sent for me, Korgan Sentar Ero Shan?' he asked.

'Come in, Herlak,' said Ero Shan. Then he turned to me. 'Herlak will serve and guard you until the result of the examination is announced. You will find him an efficient and pleasant companion.

'Herlak,' he continued, addressing my guard, 'this man is a stranger in Havatoo. He has just been before the examining board. You will be responsible for him until the board's decision has been announced. His name is Carson Napier.'

The man inclined his head. 'I understand,' he said.

'You will both dine with me in an hour,' Ero Shan announced as he took his departure.

'If you would like to rest before dinner,' said Herlak, 'there is a couch in the next room.'

I went in and lay down, and Herlak came and sat in a chair in the same room. It was evident that he was not going to let me get out of his sight. I was tired but not sleepy; so I started a conversation with Herlak.

'Are you employed in Ero Shan's house?' I asked.

'I am a soldier in the unit he commands,' he explained.

'An officer?'

'No, a common soldier.'

'But he asked you to dine with him. In my world officers do not mingle socially with common soldiers.'

Herlak laughed. 'Similar social conditions prevailed in Havatoo ages ago,' he said, 'but not now. There are no social distinctions. We are all far too intelligent, too cultured, and too sure of ourselves to need artificial conventions to determine our importance. Whether a man cleans a street or is a member of the Sanjong is not so important as is how he performs the duties of his position, his civic morality, and his culture.

'In a city where all are intelligent and cultured all men must be more or less companionable, and an officer suffers no loss of authority by mingling with his men socially.'

'But don't the soldiers take advantage of this familiarity to impose upon their officers?' I asked.

Herlak looked his surprise. 'Why should they?' he demanded. 'They know their duties as well as the officer knows his; and it is the aim in life of every good citizen to do his duty, not to evade it.'

I shook my head as I thought of the mess that earth men have made of government and civilization by neglecting to apply to the human race the simple rules which they observe to improve the breeds of dogs and cows and swine.

'Do the various classes mingle to the extent of intermarrying?' I asked.

'Of course,' replied Herlak. 'It is thus that we maintain the high moral and mental standards of the people. Were it otherwise, the yorgans must deteriorate, while the several other classes diverged so greatly from one another that eventually they would have nothing in common and no basis for mutual understanding and regard. Then must come misunderstanding, dissension, strife, and the certain destruction of the race.'

I could not but think of these very conditions on earth that had been brought about by ages of inequality of breeding, and pray that there might arise in my own world a Mankar the Bloody.

We talked of many things during that hour while we awaited dinner, and this common soldier of Havatoo discussed the sciences and the arts with far greater understanding and appreciation than I myself possessed. I asked him if he were particularly well educated, and he said that he was not – that all the men and women of Havatoo were schooled alike to a certain point, when a series of elaborate examinations determined the calling for which they were best fitted and in which they would find the greatest happiness.

'But where do you find your street cleaners?' I asked.

'You speak as though some reproach might attach to that calling,' he remonstrated.

'But it is work that many might find distasteful,' I argued.

'Necessary and useful work is never distasteful to the man best fitted to do it. Of course highly intelligent people prefer creative work, and so these necessary but more or less mechanical duties, which, by the way, are usually done by means of mechanical contrivances in Havatoo, never become the permanent calling of any man. Anyone can do them; so every onc takes his turn – that is every one in the yorgan class. It is his contribution to the public welfare – a tax paid in useful labor.'

And now a girl came to summon us to dinner. She was a very lovely girl; her saronglike garment, of fine material; her ornaments, of great beauty.

'A member of Ero Shan's family?' I asked Herlak after she had left.

'She is employed in his house,' replied Herlak. 'Korgan Sentar Ero Shan has no family.'

I had heard this Korgan Sentar title attached to Ero Shan's name previously, and had wondered relative to its significance. The two words mean warrior biologist, but they made no sense to me as a title. I questioned Herlak concerning them as we crossed the garden in response to the summons to dinner.

'The title means that he is both a warrior and a biologist; he has passed examinations admitting him to both classes. The fact that he is a member of one of the other four classes as well as a Korgan makes him an officer and eligible to the title. We common soldiers would not care to serve under any but a brilliant man; and believe me it takes a brilliant man to pass the entrance examination to any of the scientific classes, for he has to pass creditably even in the three to which he is not seeking elevation.'

Herlak led me to a large apartment where I saw Ero

Shan, three other men, and six women laughing and talking together. There was a suggestion of a lull in the conversation as we entered the room, and interested glances were cast in my direction. Ero Shan came forward to meet me and then introduced me to his other guests, who greeted me pleasantly.

As I recall them, they were Ambad Agon, Kalto Bo Gasto, and Yorgan Danar, the three men; the women were Luan, Gara Lo, Hambi Kan, Oroso, Kabell, and Joran. The men were handsome, the women beautiful; and all were intelligent and cultured, although several were of the yorgan class.

At dinner I was seated between Luan and Gara Lo, both of whom were extremely gracious. Never before in my life had I been present at such a brilliant gathering. The scintillant wit, the easy flowing conversation seemed as natural and effortless as breathing. There was no straining for effect, no labored jokes; and oftentimes there were silences. No one seemed to feel that it was necessary to speak unless there was something to say, and the silences were never strained nor embarrassing.

Luan asked me about the country from which I came, and when I told her that I was from another world, she asked me to explain how there could be another world and where.

Very briefly I explained what our astronomers had learned of the solar system. The distances staggered her.

'Twenty-six million miles!' she exclaimed, when I told her of the distance that separated Amtor from my own Earth.

Then I told her about the stars, the other suns far out in space, and that the nearest one was 255 million miles away. By this time every one at the table was listening.

'Our scientists have long known,' said Luan, 'that the old theory that Amtor is a disc floating on a sea of molten rock is wrong; they have been feeling vaguely toward something such as you describe. Your scientists must be very brilliant to have arrived at such a theory and then, as you have told me, proved it beyond question.'

'They have a great advantage over your scientists in such matters,' I explained. 'They can see the other planets and the stars by night and the sun by day; their world is not perpetually surrounded by clouds, as is Amtor.'

'Did you tell the examining board these things today?' she asked.

'They did not ask me,' I replied.

'They must not destroy you!' she exclaimed. 'Perhaps you hold the key to many secrets for which they have been searching through the ages.'

'You think they may destroy me?' I asked.

'How may I know what even the examining board may not know as yet?'

CHAPTER 13

A Professor of Astronomy

Despite the fact that my fate hung in the balance I slept soundly that night. Herlak slept on a couch near me. I called him the death watch, and he was polite enough to seem to enjoy my little joke.

Ero Shan, Herlak, and I breakfasted together the next morning. The girl who had summoned us to dinner the night before waited on us. She was so radiantly beautiful that it was almost embarrassing; I felt that I should be waiting on her. She was young, but then every one I had seen in Havatoo appeared young.

Of course I was not greatly surprised by this, for I knew of the longevity serum developed by the scientists of Amtor. I myself had been inoculated against old age, but I remarked on it casually to Ero Shan.

'Yes,' he said, 'we could live forever if the Sanjong so decreed. At least we would never die of old age or disease, but they have decreed otherwise. Our serum gives immunity for two or three hundred years, depending upon the natural constitution of the individual. When it ceases to be effective, death comes quickly. As a rule we anticipate it when we see that the end is coming.'

'But why not live forever if you can?' I asked.

'It was quite apparent that if we lived forever the number of children that could be permitted would be too small to result in any considerable improvement of the race, and so we have refused immortality in the interest of future generations and of all Amtor.'

As we were finishing breakfast, word was brought to Ero Shan directing him to bring me before the examining board immediately; and a short time later, with Herlak accompanying us, we entered Ero Shan's car and drove down the Korgan Lat, or Avenue of Warriors, toward the Central Laboratories that stand in the civic center of Havatoo.

Both Ero Shan and Herlak were unusually quiet and grave during the drive, and I sensed that they anticipated that the worst was about to befall me. Nor can I say that I was particularly blithe, though the least of my worries was occasioned by what lay in store for me; it was Duare that I was thinking of, Duare and Nalte.

The stately government buildings, the Sera Tartum, or Central Laboratories as they call them, looked very beautiful in the gorgeous setting of Mankar Pol, the park that is named for the great last jong of Havatoo, as we drove in and stopped before the building in which I had been examined the day before.

The naming of these building laboratories explains tersely their psychology of government. They have made a science of the business of governing; but research and experimentation continue, and scientists carry on such work in laboratories. I like the idea, and I recommend it to earth men; not merely the name but the application of science to the betterment of the human race and the conditions under which it lives.

We did not have to wait after we entered the building, but were immediately ushered into the presence of the examining board. Their grave faces portended bad news, and I prepared myself for the worst. Through my mind raced plans for escape, but something told me that these people did things so well and were so efficient that there would be no escape from whatever fate they decreed for me.

Kantum Shogan, chief of the board, invited me to be seated; and I took a chair facing the august five. Ero Shan sat at my right, Herlak at my left.

'Carson Napier,' commenced Kantum Shogan, 'our examination of you discovers that you are not without merit. Physically you approach that perfection toward which our race is constantly striving; intellectually you are alert but ill trained - you have no culture. While that might be remedied, I regret to advise you that you possess inherent psychological faults that, if transmitted to progeny or allowed to contaminate others through association with you, would work inestimable wrong on future generations.

'You are the unfortunate victim of inherited repressions, complexes, and fears. To a great extent you have risen above these destructive characteristics, but the chromosomes of your germ cells are replete with these vicious genes, constituting a potential menace to generations yet unborn.

'With deep regret, therefore, we could but conclude that

it would best serve the interests of humanity were you destroyed.'

'May I ask,' I inquired, 'by what right you elect to say whether or not I shall live? I am not a citizen of Havatoo. I did not come to Havatoo of my own free will. If ——'

Kantum Shogan raised his hand in a gesture that enjoined silence. 'I repeat,' he said, 'that we regret the necessity, but really there is nothing more to be said upon the subject. Your accomplishments are not such as to outweigh your inherent defects. This is unfortunate, but of course Havatoo cannot be expected to suffer because of it.'

So I was to die! After all that I had passed through it verged upon the ridiculous that I should die thus tamely simply because one of my ancestors failed to exercise a little intelligence in the selection of his bride. And to come all this long way just to die! It made me smile.

'Why do you smile?' inquired a member of the board. 'Does death seem an amusing thing to you, or do you smile because you expect to escape death through some ruse?'

'I smile,' I replied, 'when perhaps I should weep – weep at the thought of all the toil and knowledge and energy that were wasted to transport me twenty-six million miles just to die because five men of another world believe that I have inherited some bad genes.'

'Twenty-six million miles!' exclaimed a member of the board; and a second, 'Another world! What do you mean?'

'I mean that I came here from another world twenty-six million miles from Amtor,' I replied, 'a world much further advanced in some respects than yours.'

Every member of the board evinced keen interest in my statement. I heard one of them remark to another, 'This bears out the theory that many of us have long held.' 'Most interesting, and not improbable,' said another. 'I should like to hear more.'

'You say that Amtor is not the only world?' demanded Kantum Shogan, 'that there is another?'

'The heavens are filled with countless worlds,' I replied. 'Your world and mine and at least eight other worlds revolve around a great ball of flaming gases that we call a sun, and this sun with its worlds or planets is called a solar system. The illimitable void of the heavens is starred with countless other suns, many of which are the centers of other solar systems; and no man knows how many worlds there are.'

'Wait!' said Kantum Shogan. 'You have said enough to suggest that our examination of you may have been faulty in that it presumed that we possessed the sum total of available human knowledge. Now it appears that you may possess knowledge of such vast importance as to outweigh the biological inadequacies inherent in you.

'We shall question you further upon the subject of this theory which you have propounded, and in the meantime the execution of our sentence is postponed. Our final decision as to your future will depend upon the outcome of this further questioning. Science may ignore no possible source of knowledge, and if your theory be sound and open a new field to science, you shall be free to enjoy Havatoo for life; nor shall you go unhonored.'

Although I had graduated with honors from a college of high scholastic standing, I realized as I stood in the presence of these super-men of science that what Kantum Shogan had said of me was true. By comparison with them I was poorly trained and uncultured – my degrees meaningless, my diploma a mere scrap of paper. Yet in one field of science I surpassed them, and as I explained the solar system and drew diagrams of it for them, I saw the keen interest and the ready understanding with which they grasped all that I said.

Now, for the first time, they were listening to an explanation of the phenomena of the transition from day to night and from night to day, of the seasons, of the tides. Their vision restricted by the cloud envelopes that constantly enshroud Venus, they had been able to see nothing upon which to base a planetary theory; and so it is not strange that astronomy was an unknown science to them, that the sun and the stars did not exist insofar as they were concerned.

For four hours they listened to me and questioned me; then they instructed Ero Shan and Herlak to withdraw to an anteroom with me and wait there until we were again summoned.

We did not have long to wait. In less than fifteen minutes we were recalled before the board.

'It is our unanimous opinion,' announced Kantum Shogan, 'that your value to humanity far outweighs the danger that it incurs from your inherited defects, You are to live and enjoy the freedom of Havatoo. Your duties will consist in instructing others in that new science which you call astronomy and applying it for the welfare of humanity.

'As you are now the only member of your class you may live in any section of the city you choose. Your requisitions for all that you require for your personal needs and the advancement of your department will be honored by the Sera Tartum.

'For the time being I recommend you to the guidance of Korgan Sentar Ero Shan, as you are a stranger to Havatoo and will wish to become familiar with our customs and our manners.' With that he dismissed us.

'Before I go, may I ask what is to become of the girl, Nalte, who was taken with me yesterday?' I inquired.

'She was considered fit to remain in the yorgan section of Havatoo,' he replied. 'When her duties have been definitely determined and her living quarters assigned her, I will let you know where you may find her.'

It was with a feeling of relief that I left the Sera Tartum with Ero Shan and Herlak. Nalte was safe, and so was I. Now if I could only find Duare!

I spent the following several days familiarizing myself with the city and purchasing such things as I required, all of which were suggested by Ero Shan. Among them was a car. It was very easy – all I had to do was sign a voucher.

'But what check have they on my expenditures?' I asked my friend. 'I do not even know how much has been placed to my credit.'

'Why should they check what you spend?' he asked.

'But I might be dishonest. I might buy things for which I had no need and resell them,' I suggested.

Ero Shan laughed. 'They know you will not do that,' he assured me. 'If the psychologist who examined you had not known that you are an honorable man, not even your knowledge of astronomy would have saved you; that is one vice that we will not tolerate in Havatoo. When Mankar destroyed the corrupt and the vicious, he almost completely eradicated the breeds in Havatoo, and during the many generations of men that have followed him, we have succeeded in completing the work that he inaugurated. There are no dishonest men in Havatoo.'

I often talked with Ero Shan about Duare. I wanted to

cross the river to Kormor and search for her, but he convinced me that it would be suicidal to attempt it. And in view of the fact that I had no reason to believe that she was there, I put the idea from me.

'If I had an aëroplane,' I said, 'I would find a way to search Kormor.'

'What is an aëroplane?' asked Ero Shan, and when I explained it, he became very much interested, as flying has never been developed in Amtor, at least in those portions with which I am familiar.

The idea intrigued my companion to such an extent that he could scarcely talk of anything else. I explained the various types of both heavier- and lighter-than-air ships and described the rocket in which I had traversed space from the earth to Venus. In the evening he had me sketch the several types I had explained. His interest seemed to be becoming an obsession.

One evening when I returned to the house I now shared with Ero Shan, I found a message awaiting me. It was from an under clerk of the board of examiners and gave me the address of the house in which Nalte lived.

As I was now familiar with the city, I started out in my car after the evening meal to visit Nalte. I went alone, as Ero Shan had another engagement. I think that it was with Gara Lo, one of the girls I had met at his dinner the evening of the day that I had been brought to Havatoo.

I found the house in which Nalte lived in the yorgan section on a quiet street not far from the Korgan Lat, the Avenue of Warriors. The house was occupied by women who cleaned the preparatory schools on the Korgan Lat nearby. One of their number admitted me and said that she would call Nalte; then she conducted me to a living room in which were eight or ten women. One of them was playing a musical instrument, the others were painting, embroidering, or reading.

As I entered, they stopped what they were doing and greeted me pleasantly. There was not one among them that was not beautiful, and all were intelligent and cultured. These were the scrub women of Havatoo! Breeding had done for the people of Havatoo what it has done for our prize-winning dairy herds; it had advanced them all toward perfection.

Nalte was glad to see me, and as I wished to visit with her alone I asked her to come for a ride with me.

'I am glad that you passed your examination successfully,' I said as we started toward the Korgan Lat.

Nalte laughed joyously. 'I just squeezed through,' she admitted. 'I wonder what they would say back in Andoo if they knew that I, the daughter of their jong, was considered fit only to scrub floors in Havatoo!' and again she laughed happily. It was plain to be seen that her pride had not suffered by reason of her assignment. 'But after all,' she continued, 'it is a high honor to be considered fit to remain on any footing among such a race of super-men.

'And you! I am very proud of you, Carson Napier, for I have been told that you were elevated to a high place among them.'

It was my turn to laugh now. 'I did not pass the examination at all,' I admitted. 'I would have been destroyed but for my knowledge of a science that is unknown to Amtor. It was rather a jolt to my self-esteem.'

We drove along the Korgan Lat, through the great public park and parade ground in the center of which stands a magnificent stadium, and thus to the Avenue of the Gates, which forms a great arc nearly eight miles long just inside the outer wall on the land side of Havatoo.

Here are the factories and the shops in the district included between the Avenue of Gates and the Yorgan Lat, a wide avenue a third of a mile inside the wall, all the principal shops being located along the Avenue of Gates. The avenue and the shops were brilliantly lighted, the streets swarmed with vehicles, and the walkways at the level of the second stories were crowded with pedestrians.

We drove twice the full length of the avenue, enjoying the life and beauty of the scene; then we drove into one of the parking places, to which all of the ground floors on the main arteries are devoted, and were lifted by an escalator to the walkway on the level above.

Here shops displayed their wares in show windows, much as is the custom in American cities, though many of the displays aimed solely to please the eye rather than to call attention to the goods for sale within.

The scientists of Havatoo have developed a light that is brilliant and at the same time soft, with which they attain effects impossible of achievement by our relatively crude lighting methods. At no place is the source of the light apparent; it casts soft shadows and gives forth no heat. Ordinarily it resembles sunlight, but they also produce soft, pastel shades of various hues.

After we had enjoyed the spectacle for an hour, mingling with the happy crowd upon the walkway, I made a few small purchases, including a gift for Nalte; then we returned to my car, and I took my companion home.

I was busy the next morning organizing my classes in astronomy, and so numerous were those wishing to enroll that I had to organize several large classes, and as only four hours a day is ordinarily devoted to work of any nature, it was evident that I should have to devote my time at first to the training of instructors, if the new science were to be expounded to all that were interested.

I was greatly flattered by the personnel of the first matriculants. Not only were there scientists and soldiers from the first five classes of Havatoo; but every member of the Sanjong, the ruling quintumvirate of Havatoo, enrolled. The thirst of these people for useful knowledge is insatiable.

Shortly after noon, my work for the day having been completed, I received a summons to call upon Korgan Kantum Mohar, the warrior physicist who had arranged for the examination of Nalte and me the day that Ero Shan had brought us to the city.

I could not but wonder what he wanted of me. Could it be that I must undergo another examination? Always, I presume, I shall connect Mohar's name with examinations.

As I entered his office on the Sera Tartum, he greeted me with the same pleasant demeanor that had marked his attitude the day that he had told me that I was to be examined to ascertain whether or not I should be permitted to live; so his graciousness was not entirely reassuring.

'Come over here and sit down near me,' he said. 'I have something here that I should like to discuss with you.'

As I took a chair beside him, I saw spread on his desk the sketches of airships that I had made for Ero Shan.

'These,' he said, pointing to the sketches, 'were brought to me by Ero Shan, who explained them as best he could. He was quite excited and enthusiastic about them, and I must confess that he imparted some of his enthusiasm to me.

I am much interested, and would know more concerning these ships that sail through the air.'

For an hour I talked to him and answered his questions. I dwelt principally on the practical achievements of aëronautics – the long flights, the great speed, the uses to which ships had been put in times of peace and in times of war.

Korgan Kantum Mohar was deeply interested. The questions that he asked revealed the trained, scientific mind; and the last one that of the soldier, the man of action.

'Can you build one of these ships for me?' he demanded.

I told him that I could, but that it might require long experimentation to adapt their motors and materials to the requirements of a successful aëroplane.

'You have two or three hundred years,' he said with a smile, 'and the resources of a race of scientists. Materials that we do not now possess, we can produce; nothing is impossible to science.'

CHAPTER 14

The Attack in the Night

I was given a factory close to the Tag kum voo Klookantum, the Gate of the Physicists, at the end of Kantum Lat. I chose this location because there was a level plain beyond this gate that would make an excellent flying field, and also so that I would have my finished plane finally assembled where it could easily be wheeled out of the city without interfering with traffic to any great extent.

On the advice of the Sanjong, which took a deep interest in both this new venture into aeronautics and the, to them, new science of astronomy, I divided my time between the two.

My time was fully occupied, and I worked far more than the usual four hours a day. But I enjoyed the work, especially the building of a plane; and engrossing were the day dreams in which I indulged of exploring Venus in a ship of my own.

The necessity for relaxation and entertainment is stressed by the people of Havatoo, and Ero Shan was constantly dragging me away from my drawing board or my conferences with the corps of assistants that had been placed at my disposal by Mohar to take me to this thing or that.

There were theaters, art exhibits, lectures, musicales, concerts, and games of various descriptions in gymnasiums and the great stadium. Many of their games are extremely dangerous, and injury and death often accompany them. In the great stadium at least once a month men fight with wild beasts or with one another to the death, and once a year the great war game is played. Ero Shan, Gara Lo, Nalte, and I attended this year's game together. To Nalte and I it was all new; we did not know what to expect.

'Probably we shall witness an exhibition of such scientific wonders as only the men of Havatoo are capable,' I suggested to her.

'I haven't the faintest conception of what it will be,' she replied. 'No one will tell me anything about it. They say,

"Wait and see. You will be thrilled as you have never been before." '

'The game doubtless hinges on the use of the most modern, scientific instruments of war and strategy,' I ventured.

'Well,' she remarked, 'we shall soon know. It is about time for the games to commence.'

The great stadium, seating two hundred thousand people, was crammed to capacity. It was gorgeous with the costumes and the jewels of the women and the handsome trappings of the men, for the intelligence of Havatoo concedes their full value to beauty and to art. But of all that went to make up this splendid spectacle, there was nothing more outstanding than the divine beauty of the people themselves.

Suddenly a cry arose, a roar of welcome. 'They come! They come! The warriors come!'

Onto the field at each end marched a hundred men, a hundred men naked but for white G strings at one end of the field, a hundred men naked but for red G strings at the other end of the field. They carried short swords and shields. For a while they stood inactive, waiting; then two small cars were driven onto the field. Each contained a driver and a young woman; that is, they looked young. Of course they might have been anywhere from eighteen to three hundred years old, for the people of Havatoo do not age after maturity; I mean they do not age in appearance.

One of the cars was red, the other white. The red car attached itself to the contingent wearing the red G strings, the white car to the whites.

When they were in position, the two factions paraded entirely around the field clockwise. As they passed the stands, the people cheered and shouted words of encouragement and praise, and when the warriors had completed the circuit they took their places again at each end of the field.

Presently a trumpet sounded, and the reds and the whites approached one another. Now their formations were changed. There were an advance party and a rear guard, there were flankers on either side. The cars remained in the rear, just in front of the rear guard. On running boards that encircled the cars were a number of warriors.

I leaned toward Ero Shan. 'Tell us something of the idea of the game,' I begged, 'so that we may understand and enjoy it better.'

'It is simple,' he replied. 'They contend for fifteen vir (that is equivalent to sixty minutes of earth time), and the side that captures the opponent's queen oftener is the winner.'

I do not know what I expected but certainly not that which followed. The reds formed a wedge with its apex toward the whites and charged. In the mêlée that ensued I saw three men killed and more than a dozen wounded, but the whites held their queen.

When a queen was pressed too closely, her car turned and fled, the rear guard coming up to repel the enemy. The tide of battle moved up and down the field. Sometimes the whites seemed about to capture the red queen, again their own was in great danger. There were many individual duels and a display of marvellous swordsmanship throughout.

But the whole thing seemed so out of harmony with all that I had heretofore seen in Havatoo that I could find no explanation for it. Here was the highest type of culture and civilization that man might imagine suddenly reverting to barbarism. It was inexplicable. And the strangest part of all of it to me was the almost savage enjoyment with which the people viewed the bloody spectacle.

I must admit that I found it thrilling, but I was glad when it was over. Only one queen was captured during the entire game. At the very last the red queen fell into the hands of the whites, but only after the last of her defenders had fallen.

Of the two hundred men who took part in the game not one came through unwounded; fifty were killed on the field, and I afterward learned that ten more died of their wounds later.

As we drove from the stadium toward our house, I asked Ero Shan how such a savage and brutal exhibition could be tolerated, much less enjoyed, by the refined and cultured inhabitants of Havatoo.

'We have few wars,' he replied. 'For ages war was man's natural state. It gave expression to the spirit of adventure that is a part of his inheritance. Our psychologists discovered that man must have some outlet for this age-old urge. If it be not given him by wars or dangerous games, he will seek it in the commission of crimes, or in quarrels with his fellows. It is better that it is so. Without it man would stagnate, he would die of ennui.'

So that was that. It seemed a strange philosophy; but I was bound to accept it, as I had come to accept everything born of the wisdom of Havatoo.

I was now working on my plane with the keenest enthusiasm, for I now saw rapidly taking form such a ship as, I truly believe, might be built nowhere in the universe other than in Havatoo. Here I had at my disposal materials that only the chemists of Havatoo might produce, synthetic wood and steel and fabric that offered incalculable strength and durability combined with negligible weight.

I had also the element, vik-ro, undiscovered on earth, and the substance, lor, to furnish fuel for my engine. The action of the element, vik-ro, upon the element, yor-san, which is contained in the substance, lor, results in absolute annihilation of the lor. Some conception of the amount of energy thus released may be obtained by considering the fact that there is eighteen thousand million times as much energy liberated by the *annihilation* of a ton of coal as by its *combustion.* Fuel for the life of my ship could be held in the palm of my hand, and with the materials that entered into its construction the probable life of the ship was computed by the physicists working on it to be in the neighborhood of fifty years. Can you wonder that I looked forward with impatience to the completion of such a marvel ship!

At last it was finished! I spent the final afternoon checking it over carefully with my large corps of assistants. On the morrow it was to be wheeled out through the Tag kum voo Klookantum for my trial flight. I knew that it would be successful. All my assistants knew that it would be; it was a scientific certainty that it must fly.

That evening I determined to indulge in a little relaxation; and I called Nalte on the wireless, transmitterless, receiverless communicating system that is one of the wonders of Havatoo. I asked her if she would take dinner with me, and she accepted with an alacrity and display of pleasure that warmed my heart.

We dined in a little public garden on the roof of a building at the corner of Yorgan Lat and Havatoo Lat just inside the river wall at the lower end of Havatoo Lat, the avenue that extends along the water front.

'It seems good to see you again,' said Nalte. 'It has been

a long time – not since the war games. I thought you had forgotten me.'

'Far from it,' I assured her, 'but I have been working day and night on my airship.'

'I have heard some mention of it,' she said, 'but no one that I have talked with seemed to understand very much about it. Just what is it, and what will it do?'

'It is a ship that flies through the air faster than a bird can fly,' I replied.

'But what good will that be?' she demanded.

'It will carry people quickly and safely from one place to another,' I explained.

'You don't mean to say that people will ride in it!' she exclaimed.

'Why certainly; why else should I build it? That is what it is for.'

'But what will keep it in the air? Will it flap its wings like a bird?'

'No; it will soar like a bird on stationary wings.'

'But how will you get through the forests where the trees grow close together?'

'I shall fly over the forests.'

'So high? Oh, it will be dangerous,' she cried. 'Please do not go up in it, Carson Napier.'

'It will be very safe,' I assured her, 'much safer than incurring the dangers of the forests on foot. No savage beasts nor savage men can harm the voyager in an airship.'

'But think of being way up above the trees!' she cried with a little shudder.

'I shall fly even higher than that,' I told her. 'I shall fly over the loftiest mountains.'

'But you will never fly over the great trees of Amtor; I know that,' she stated emphatically.

She referred to the gigantic trees that raise their lofty tips five thousand feet above the surface of Amtor to drink the moisture from the inner cloud envelope.

'Yes; possibly I shall fly even above those,' I replied, 'though I will admit that flying blind in that solid bank of cloud does not appeal to me.'

She shook her head. 'I shall be afraid every time I know that you are up in the thing.'

'Oh, no, you won't, not after you are familiar with it. Some day soon I am going to take you up with me.'

'Unh, unh!' she negatived. 'Not I.'

'We could fly to Andoo,' I said. 'I have been thinking of that ever since I started to build the ship.'

'To Andoo!' she exclaimed. 'Home! Oh, Carson, if we only could!'

'But we can – that is if we can find Andoo. The ship will take us anywhere. If we could carry enough food and water, we could stay in the air for fifty years, and it certainly wouldn't take that long to find Andoo.'

'I love it here in Havatoo,' she said, musingly, 'but after all home is home. I want to see my own people, but I would like to come back to Havatoo again. That is, if ——'

'If what?' I asked.

'If you are going to be here.'

I reached across the table and pressed her hand. 'We *have* been pretty good friends, haven't we, Nalte? I should miss you terribly if I thought that I were not to see you again.'

'I think that you are the best friend that I ever had,' she said, and then she looked up at me quickly and laughed. 'Do you know,' she continued; but stopped suddenly and looked down, as a slight flush suffused her cheeks.

'Do I know what?' I asked.

'Well, I might as well confess. There was a long time that I thought that I loved you.'

'That would have been a great honor, Nalte.'

'I tried to hide it because I knew that you loved Duare; and now recently Ero Shan has been coming to see me, and I know that I did not know before what love was.'

'You love Ero Shan?'

'Yes.'

'I am glad. He is a splendid fellow. I know that you will both be happy.'

'That might be true but for one thing,' she said.

'And what is that?'

'Ero Shan does not love me.'

'How do you know that he doesn't? I don't see how he could help it. If I had never know Duare ——'

'If he loved me, he would tell me,' she interrupted. 'Sometimes I think that he believes that I belong to you. We came here together, you know; and we have been much together since. But what's the good in speculating! If he loved me, he would not be able to hide it.'

We had finished our dinner, and I suggested that we drive about the city for a while and then go to a concert.

'Let's take a little walk instead of driving,' suggested Nalte, and as we rose from our table, 'How beautiful the view is from here!'

In the strange glow of the Amtorian night the expanse of the great river stretched into the vanishing visibility above and below the city, while on the opposite shore gloomy Kormor was but a darker blotch against the darkness of the night, with here and there a few dim lights showing feebly in contrast to brilliant Havatoo lying at our feet.

We followed the walkway along Havatoo Lat to a narrow side street that extended away from the river. 'Let's turn here,' said Nalte. 'I feel like quiet and dim lights tonight, not the brilliance and the crowds of Havatoo Lat.'

The street that we turned into was in the yorgan section of the city; it was but dimly lighted, and the walkway was deserted. It was a quiet and restful street even by comparison with the far from noisy main avenues of Havatoo, where raucous noises are anathema.

We had proceeded but a short distance from Havatoo Lat when I heard a door that we had passed open behind us and footsteps on the walkway. I gave the matter no thought, in fact I scarcely had time to give it thought when someone seized me roughly from behind, and as I wheeled about I saw another man grab Nalte, clap a hand over her mouth, and drag her into the doorway from which the two had come.

CHAPTER 15

The City of the Dead

I tried to break away from the man that held me, but he was very strong. I did, however, succeed in turning about so that I could strike him; and this I did repeatedly, hitting him in the face as he sought to reach my throat with his fingers.

We must have made quite a lot of noise in that quiet street, although neither of us spoke, for soon a head was put out of a window, and presently men and women came running from their houses. But before any of them reached us I had tripped my assailant and was on top of him clutching his throat. I should have choked the life out of him had not several men dragged me from him.

They were shocked and angry because of this unseemly disturbance and brawl on a street in Havatoo; and they placed us under arrest, nor would they listen to what I tried to tell them.

'The judges will listen to you,' was all that they would say; 'it is not our province to judge.'

As every citizen of Havatoo has police powers, and there is no other police force, there was no delay as there would have been in an earthly city while waiting for the police to answer a summons.

We were bundled into a large car belonging to one of the citizens, and with an adequate guard we were whisked away toward the Sera Tartum.

They do things with celerity in Havatoo. They may have a jail; I presume they have, but they didn't waste any time or cause the state any expense by putting us in to be boarded and lodged by the taxpayers.

Five men were hastily summoned, one from each of the upper classes; they were judge, jury, and court of last resort. They sat in a large room that resembled a huge library; they were served by a dozen clerks.

One of the judges asked us our names, and when we had given them two clerks went quickly to the shelves and brought forth books in which they commenced to search.

Then the judges asked those who had arrested us to explain why they brought us in. During the recital of our violation of the peace of Havatoo one of the clerks, evidently having found what he sought, laid his book open before the judges; the other was still searching.

From the open book one of the judges read aloud my official record since I had come to Havatoo, including the result of the examination that I had undergone and its embarrassing finding.

A judge asked me to state my case. In a few brief words I told of the unprovoked attack upon us and the abduction of Nalte, and in conclusion I said, 'Instead of wasting time trying me for being the victim of this unwarranted attack and defending myself against my assailant, you should be helping me search for the girl who has been stolen.'

'The peace of Havatoo is of more importance than the life of any individual,' replied a judge. 'When we have fixed the responsibility for this breach of the peace, the other matter will be investigated.'

The second clerk now approached the judges. 'The name of the prisoner who calls himself Mal Un does not appear in the records of Havatoo.'

All eyes turned toward my assailant, Mal Un, and for the first time I had a good look at him under a bright light. I saw his eyes! Instantly I recalled, what evidently I had noticed only subconsciously before – the chill of the flesh of his hands and his throat when I had fought with him. And now those eyes! They were the eyes of a dead man.

I wheeled toward the judges. 'I understand it all now,' I cried. 'When I first came to Havatoo, I was told that there were few bad men in the city; but that occasionally, none knew how, bad men came from the city of Kormor across the river and stole men and women from Havatoo. This man is from Kormor. He is not a living man; he is a corpse. He and his companion sought to steal Nalte and me for Skor!'

With calm efficiency the judges made a few brief and simple, but none the less effective, tests upon Mal Un; then they whispered together for a few seconds without leaving the bench. Following this he who acted as spokesman for the tribunal cleared his throat.

'Mal Un,' he announced, 'you will be decapitated and

cremated forthwith. Carson Napier, you are exonerated with honor. You are free. You may conduct a search for your companion and call upon any citizen of Havatoo to assist you in any way that you desire assistance.'

As I was leaving the room I heard a mirthless laugh burst from the dead mouth of Mal Un. Horribly it rang in my ears as I hastened out into the night. The dead man laughing because he was sentenced to death!

Naturally, the first person I thought of in my extremity was Ero Shan. My own car was parked where I had left it at the corner of Yorgan Lat and Havatoo Lat; so I hailed a public conveyance and was driven rapidly to the house at which Ero Shan was being entertained that evening.

I did not go in but sent word that I wished to speak to him upon a matter of great urgency, and a moment later I saw him coming from the house toward me.

'What brings you here, Carson?' he asked. 'I thought that you were spending the evening with Nalte.'

When I told him what had happened, he went very white. 'There is no time to be lost!' he cried. 'Can you find that house again?'

I told him that I could. 'That doorway is indelibly burned into my memory.'

'Dismiss your car; we will go in mine,' he said, and a moment later we were speeding toward the place where I had lost Nalte.

'You have all my sympathy, my friend,' said Ero Shan. 'To have lost the woman you love, and such a woman! is a calamity beyond any feeble words to express.'

'Yes,' I replied, 'and even if I had loved Nalte, I could scarcely be more grieved than I now am.'

' "Even if you had loved Nalte"!' he repeated incredulously. 'But, man, you do love her, do you not?'

'We were only the best of friends,' I replied. 'Nalte did not love me.'

Ero Shan made no reply; he but drove swiftly on in silence. Presently we reached our destination. The section of the street in which the house we sought stood, being very close to a heavily travelled main artery, accommodated pedestrian traffic on elevated walkways, unlike residential districts farther removed from heavy vehicular traffic.

Ero Shan stopped his car beside the stairway, nearest the

house, that led up to the walkway; and a moment later we were before the door. Repeated summons elicited no response, and then I tried the door and found it unlocked.

Together we entered the dark interior, and I regretted that we had brought no weapons; but in peaceful Havatoo men do not ordinarily go armed. Ero Shan soon located a light switch, and as the room in which we stood was illuminated, we saw that it was entirely unfurnished.

The building rose two stories above the walkway, and of course there was a lower floor on a level with the street. We searched the upper stories first and then the roof, for in this part of Havatoo most of the roofs are developed as gardens; but we found no sign of recent habitation. Then we went to the ground floor, but with no better results. Here was space for the parking of cars and in rear of that a number of dark storerooms.

'There is no living creature in this house except ourselves,' said Ero Shan. 'They must have taken Nalte to some other house. It will be necessary to make a search, and only under the authority of the Sanjong itself may the home of a citizen be searched. Come! We will go and get that authority.'

'You go,' I said. 'I will remain here. We should keep a careful watch on this house.'

'You are right,' he replied. 'I shall not be gone long.'

After Ero Shan's departure I commenced another careful investigation of the premises. Once again I went through every room searching for some secret place where a person might be hidden.

I had covered the upper stories of the house thus and was searching the first floor. The dust of neglect lay heavy upon everything, but I noticed that in one of the back rooms it had been disturbed upon the floor at a point where Ero Shan and I had not walked. Previously this had escaped my notice. It seemed to me that it might be fraught with importance.

I examined the floor carefully. I saw footprints. They approached a wall; and there they stopped; there seemed to be a path worn in the dust to this point in the wall. I examined the wall. It was covered with a form of synthetic wood common in Havatoo, and when I rapped upon it, it sounded hollow.

The wall covering was applied in panels about three feet

wide, and at the top of the panel I was examining was a small round hole about an inch in diameter. Inserting a forefinger in this hole I discovered just what I had imagined I would discover – a latch. I tripped it; and with slight pressure the panel swung toward me, revealing a dark aperture beyond it.

At my feet I dimly discerned the top of a flight of steps. I listened intently; no sound came up to me from the gloom into which the stairs disappeared. Naturally, I was convinced that Nalte's abductor had carried her down that stairway.

I should have waited for the return of Ero Shan, but I thought that Nalte might be in danger. I could not think of wasting a single precious instant in delay.

I placed a foot upon the stairs and started to descend; and as I did so the panel closed softly behind me, actuated by a spring. I heard the latch lick. I was now in utter darkness. I had to feel my way. At any moment I might come upon Nalte's abductor waiting to dispatch me. It was a most uncomfortable sensation.

The stairway, which was apparently cut from the living limestone that underlies Havatoo, ran straight down to a great depth. From the bottom of the stairway I felt my way along a narrow corridor. Occasionally I stopped and listened. At first I heard not a sound; the silence was the silence of the grave.

Presently the walls commenced to feel moist; and then, occasionally, a drop of water fell upon my head. Now a low, muffled sound like the shadow of a roar seemed to fill the subterranean corridor like a vague, oppressive menace.

On and on I groped my way. I could not advance rapidly, for I was compelled to feel every forward footstep before taking it; I could not know what lay beyond the last.

Thus I continued on for a long distance until finally an extended foot felt an obstruction. Investigating, I found that it was the lowest step of a flight of stairs.

Cautiously I ascended, and at the top I came against a blank wall. But experience had taught me where to search for a latch, for I was confident that what barred my progress was a door; and doors have latches.

Presently my fingers found what they sought; a door gave

to the pressure of my hand. I pushed it slowly and cautiously until a narrow crack permitted me to look beyond it.

I saw a portion of a room dimly illuminated by the night light of Amtor. There was no one in that portion of the room that I could see. I opened the door a little farther; there was no one in the room. I stepped into it, but before I permitted the door to close, I located the opening through which the latch could be tripped from that side.

The room in which I found myself was filthy and littered with debris. It was filled with a revolting, musty odor that suggested death and decay.

In the wall opposite me were three openings, a doorway and two windows; but there was no window sash and no door. Beyond the door, to which I now crossed, was a yard enclosed by one side of the building and a high wall. This yard was in even a more untidy condition than the room, but at present I was not concerned with the yard.

There were three rooms on the ground floor of the building, and these I searched rapidly; they contained only broken furniture, old rags, and dirt. I went upstairs. Here were three more rooms; they revealed nothing more of interest than those downstairs.

Than these six rooms there was nothing more to the house, and so I was soon aware that I must search farther for Nalte. Neither she nor any one else was in this house.

From an upper window I looked out over the yard. Beyond the wall I saw a street. It was a dingy, gloomy street. The houses that fronted it were drab and dilapidated, but I did not have to look out upon this scene to know where I was. Long before this I had guessed that I was in Kormor, the city of the cruel jong of Morov. The tunnel through which I had passed from Havatoo had carried me beneath the great river that is called Gerlat kum Rov, River of Death. Now I knew that Nalte had been abducted by the agents of Skor.

From the window I saw an occasional pedestrian on the street that passed the house. They moved with slow, shuffling steps. I could not but shudder as I contemplated these gruesome figures that should long have been moldering in their graves, but I did not give myself over for long to these depressing thoughts. There was another even more terrible that assailed my mind – somewhere in that city of the dead was Nalte in danger so great that I turned cold at the mere thought of it. I must find her! But how?

Descending to the yard, I passed through a gateway in the wall out into the street. Only the natural, nocturnal light of Amtor illuminated the scene. I did not know which way to go, yet I knew that I must keep moving if I were not to attract attention.

I must admit that I felt quite helpless and inadequate to the task before me.

My judgment and my knowledge of Skor suggested that where Skor was, there I would find Nalte, and so I knew that I must find the jong's palace. If I might only stop one of the pedestrians and ask him; but that I did not dare do, for to reveal my ignorance of the location of the jong's palace would be to brand me a stranger and therefore an enemy.

I was approaching two men who were walking in the opposite direction to that which I had chosen. As I passed them I noted their somber garb, and I saw them half stop as we came abreast and eye me intently. But they did not accost me, and it was with relief that I realized later that they had gone on their way.

Now I understood that with my handsome trappings and my brisk, alert step and carriage I would be a marked man in Kormor. It became absolutely imperative, therefore, that I disguise myself; but that was going to be more easily thought of than accomplished. However, it must be done. I could never hope to find and rescue Nalte if I were constantly subject to detection and arrest.

Turning, I retraced my steps to the mean hovel I had just quitted, for there I remembered having seen odds and ends of rags and discarded clothing from among which I hoped that I might select sufficient to cover my nakedness and replace the fine apparel I had purchased in Havatoo.

Nor was I disappointed, and a few moments later I emerged again upon the street clothed in the cleanest of the foul garments I had had to select from. And now, to carry out my disguise to the fullest, I shuffled slowly along like some carrion from a forgotten grave.

Again I met pedestrians; but this time they gave me no second look, and I knew that my disguise was ample. To all outward appearances, in this unlighted city of the dead, I was just another corpse.

In a few houses dim lights burned; but I heard no noises – no singing, no laughter. The streets were filthy; and over all hung an oppressive, charnel odor. Somewhere in this city of horror was Nalte. That so sweet and lovely a creature was breathing this fetid air was sufficiently appalling, but of far greater import was the fact that her life hung in the balance.

If Skor were in the city, he might kill her quickly in a fit of mad revenge because she had escaped him once, My sustaining hope was that Skor was at his castle and that his minions would hold Nalte unharmed until he returned to Kormor. But how to learn these things!

I knew that it would be dangerous to question any of the inhabitants; but finally I realized that in no other way might I find quickly the house of Skor, and haste was essential if I were to find Nalte before it was too late.

As I wandered without plan I saw nothing to indicate that I was approaching a better section such as I felt might contain the palace of a jong. The houses were all low and grimy and unlovely.

I saw a man standing at the intersection of two streets, and as I came close to him I stopped. He looked at me with his glassy eyes.

'I am lost,' I said.

'We are all lost,' he replied, his dead tongue thick in his dead mouth.

'I cannot find the house where I live.'

'Go into any house; what difference does it make?'

'I want to find my own house,' I insisted.

'Go and find it then. How should I know where it is if you do not?'

'It is near the house of the jong,' I told him.

'Then go to the house of the jong,' he suggested surlily.

'Where is it?' I demanded in the same thick tones.

He pointed down the street that I had been following; and then he turned and shuffled away in the opposite direction, while I continued on in the direction he had indicated. I wished to reach my destination quickly; but I dared not accelerate my speed for fear of attracting attention, and so I shuffled along in the lifeless manner of the other wayfarers that I had seen.

Somewhere ahead of me lay the palace of Skor, Jong of Morov; there I was certain that I should find Nalte. But after I found her – what?

CHAPTER 16

A SURPRISE

THE palace of Skor was a three-storied building of grey stone similar in its ugliness to his castle by the river in the forest, but it was considerably larger. It stood in no spacious plaza. Mean hovels were its near neighbors. All about it was a high wall, and before heavy gates stood a dozen warriors. It looked impregnable.

I shuffled slowly past the gates, observing from the corners of my eyes. It seemed useless to attempt to enter there. The guards were posted for a purpose, and that purpose must be to keep out those who had no business within. What reason could I give for wishing to enter? – what reason that they would accept?

It was evident that I must seek some other means of ingress. If I failed to find any, then I might return to the gates as a last resort, but I can tell you that the outlook seemed almost hopeless.

I followed the high wall that enclosed the palace grounds, but nowhere did I find any place to scale it. It was about twelve feet high, just too high for me to reach the top with my fingers by a running jump.

I reached the rear of the palace without discovering any place where I might scale the wall, and I was convinced that there was no place. There were plenty of litter and rubbish in the filthy street that encircled the wall, but nothing that I could use as a ladder.

Upon the opposite side of the street were mean hovels, many of which appeared deserted. In only a few, dim lights revealed a sign of – life, I was going to say – of occupancy. Directly across from me an open door sagged on a single hinge. It gave me an idea.

I crossed the street. There were no lights in any of the nearby houses. That before which I stood appeared tenantless. Stealthily I crept to the doorway and listened. There was no sound from the gloom of the interior, but I must make sure that no one was there.

Scarcely breathing, I entered the house. It was a one-story

hovel of two rooms. I searched them both. The house was unoccupied. Then I returned to the door and examined the remaining hinge. To my delight I discovered that I could easily remove the door, and this I did.

I looked up and down the street. There was no one in sight. Lifting the door, I crossed to the wall and leaned the door against it. Again I searched the street with my eyes. All was clear.

Cautiously I crawled up the door. From its top, precariously gained, I could reach the top of the wall. Then I threw caution to the winds, drew myself up, and dropped to the ground on the opposite side. I could not take the chance of remaining even for an instant on the summit of the wall in plain view of the palace windows on one side and the street on the other.

I recalled the vicious kazars that Skor kept at his castle, and I prayed that he kept none here. But no kazar attacked me, nor did any evidence suggest that my entry had been noted.

Before me loomed the palace, dark and forbidding even though some lights shone within it. The courtyard was flagged, and as barren as that of the castle in the wood – barren of aught but refuse.

Crossing quickly to the building I walked along it, seeking an entrance. It was a three-storied building. I saw at least two towers; whether or not there are more I do not know. Many of the windows were barred, but not all. Behind one of those barred windows, perhaps, was Nalte. The task before me was to discover which.

I dared not go to the front of the palace lest I be questioned by the guard; so I was forced to find ingress elsewhere. Presently I discovered a small door; it was the only door on this side of the building, but it was securely locked. Carrying my investigation farther, I came to an open window. The room beyond was unlighted. I listened but heard no sound; then I vaulted quietly to the sill and dropped within. At last I was inside the palace of the jong of Morov.

Crossing the room, I found a door on the opposite side; and when I drew it open I saw a dimly lighted corridor beyond. And with the opening of the door sounds from the interior of the palace reached my ears.

The corridor was deserted as I stepped into it and made

my way in the direction of the sounds I had heard. At a turning I came to a broader and better lighted corridor, but here dead men and women passed to and fro. Some were carrying dishes laden with food in one direction, other were bearing empty dishes in the opposite direction.

I knew that I risked detection and exposure, but I also knew that that was a risk I must take sooner or later. As well now, I thought, as any time. I noticed that these corpses were painted in the semblance of life and health; only their eyes and their shuffling gait revealed the truth. My eyes I could not change, but I kept them lowered as I shuffled into the corridor behind a man carrying a large platter of food.

I followed him to a large room in which two score men and women were seated at a banquet table. Here at last, I thought, were living people – the masters of Kormor. They did not seem a very gay company, but that I could understand in surroundings such as theirs. The men were handsome, the women beautiful. I wondered what had brought them and what kept them in this horrid city of death.

A remarkable feature of the assemblage was the audience that packed the room, leaving only sufficient space for the servants to pass around the table. These people were so well painted that at first I thought them alive too.

Seeing an opportunity to lose my identity in the crowd, I wormed my way behind the rear rank and then gradually worked my way around the room and toward the front rank of the spectators until I stood directly in rear of a large, thronelike chair that stood at the head of the table and which I assumed to be Skor's chair.

Close contact with the men and women watching the banqueters soon disclosed the fact that I was doubtless the only living creature among them, for no make-up, however marvellous, could alter the expressionlessness of those dead eyes or call back the fire of life or the light of soul. Poor creatures! How I pitied them.

And now, from the lower end of the chamber, came a blare of trumpets; and all the banqueters arose and faced in that direction. Four trumpeters marching abreast entered the banquet hall, and behind them came eight warriors in splendid harness. Following these were a man and a woman, partially hidden from my sight by the warriors and the trumpeters marching in front of them. These two were followed by eight more warriors.

And now the trumpeters and the warriors separated and formed an aisle down which the man and the woman walked. Then I saw them and my heart stood still. Skor and – Duare! The man I loathed, the woman I loved!

Duare's head was still high – it would be difficult to break that proud spirit – but the loathing, the anguish, the hopelessness in her eyes struck me like a dagger to the heart. Yet, even so, hope bounded in my breast as I saw them, for they *were* expressions; and they told me that Skor had not yet worked his worst upon her.

They seated themselves, Skor at the head of the table, Duare at his right, scarce three paces from me; and the guests resumed their seats.

I had come for Nalte, and I had found Duare. How was I to rescue her now that I had found her? I realized that I must do nothing precipitate. Here, faced by overwhelming odds in the stronghold of an enemy, I knew that I might accomplish nothing by force. Strategy and stealth were the weapons that would avail me most.

I looked about the room. On one side were windows, in the center of the opposite wall was a small door, at the far end the large doors through which all seemed to be entering or leaving; and behind me was another small doorway. I had no plan, but it was well to note the things that I had noted.

I saw Skor pound on the table with his fist. All the guests looked up. Skor raised a goblet, and the guests did likewise.

'To the jong!' he cried.

'To the jong!' repeated the guests.

'Drink!' commanded Skor, and the guests drank.

Then Skor addressed them. It was not a speech; it was a monologue to which all listened. In it occurred what Skor evidently considered an amusing anecdote. When he had narrated it he paused, waiting. There was only silence. Skor scowled. 'Laugh!' he snapped, and the guests laughed – hollow, mirthless laughs. It was then, with those laughs, that my suspicions were aroused.

When Skor finished his monologue, there was another silence until he commanded, 'Applaud!' Skor smiled and bowed in acknowledgment of the ensuing applause just as though it had been spontaneous and genuine.

'Eat!' he commanded, and the guests ate; then he said, 'Talk!' and they commenced to converse.

'Let us be gay!' cried Skor. 'This is a happy moment for Morov. I bring you your future queen!' He pointed to Duare. There was only silence. 'Applaud!' growled Skor, and when they had done his bidding, he urged them again to be gay. 'Let us have laughter,' he bid them. 'Starting at my left you will take turns laughing, and when the laughter has passed around the table to the future queen, you will start over again.'

The laughter commenced. It rose and fell as it passed around the table. God! What a travesty on gaiety it was!

I had pressed closer until I stood directly behind Skor's chair. Had Duare turned her eyes in my direction she must have seen me, but she did not. She sat staring straight before her, avoiding the dead eyes of the horrid guests.

Skor leaned toward her and spoke. 'Are they not fine specimens?' he demanded. 'You see, I am coming closer and closer to the fulfilment of my dream. Do you not see how different are all the people of Kormor from the mean creatures at my castle? And look at these, the guests at my table. Even their eyes have the semblance of real life. Soon I shall have it – I shall be able to breathe full life into the dead. Then think what a nation I can create! And I shall be jong, and you shall be vadjong,.'

'I do not wish to be vadjong,' replied Duare dully. 'I only wish my liberty.'

A dead man sitting across the table from her said, 'That is all that any of us wishes, but we shall never get it.' It was then his turn to laugh, and he laughed. It was incongruous, horrible. I saw Duare shudder.

Skor's sallow face paled. He glowered at the speaker. 'I am about to give you life,' cried the jong angrily, 'and you do not appreciate it.'

'We do not wish to live,' replied the corpse. 'We wish death. Let us have death and oblivion – let us return to our graves in peace.'

At these words, Skor flew into a fit of rage. He half rose, and drawing a sword struck at the face of the speaker. The keen blade laid open an ugly wound from temple to chin.

The edges of the wound gaped wide, but no blood flowed.

The dead man laughed. 'You cannot hurt the dead,' he mocked.

Skor was livid. He sought words, but his rage choked him. Flecks of foam whitened his lips. If ever I have looked upon a madman, it was then. Suddenly he turned upon Duare.

'You are the cause of this!' he creamed. 'Never say such things again before my subjects. You shall be queen! I will make you queen of Morov, a living queen, or I will make you one of these. Which do you choose?'

'Give me death,' replied Duare.

'That you shall never have – not real death, only the counterfeit that you see before you—neither life nor death.'

At last the ghastly meal drew to a close. Skor arose and motioned Duare to accompany him. He did not leave the room as he had entered it; no trumpeters nor warriors accompanied him. He walked toward the small doorway at the rear of the room, the spectators giving way before him and Duare as they advanced.

So suddenly had Skor risen and turned that I thought he must surely see me; but if he did he did not recognize me, and a moment later he had passed me, and the danger was over. And as he and Duare moved toward the doorway I fell in behind and followed. Each instant I expected to feel a hand upon my shoulder stopping me, but no one seemed to pay any attention to me. I passed through the doorway behind Skor and Duare without a challenge. Even Skor did not turn as he raised the hangings at the doorway and let them fall again behind him.

I moved softly, making no noise. The corridor in which we were was deserted. It was a very short corridor, ending at a heavy door. As Skor threw this door open I saw a room beyond that at first I thought must be a storeroom. It was a large room almost completely filled with a heterogeneous collection of odds and ends of furniture, vases, clothing, arms, and pictures. Everything was confusion and disorder, and everything was covered with dust and dirt.

Skor paused for a moment on the threshold, seemingly viewing the room with pride. 'What do you think of it?' he demanded.

'Think of what?' asked Duare.

'This beautiful room,' he said. 'In all Amtor there cannot

be a more beautiful room; nowhere else can there be another such collection of beautiful objects; and now to them I am adding the most beautiful of all – you? This, Duare, is to be your room – the private apartment of the queen of Morov.'

I stepped in and closed the door behind me, for I had seen that but for us three there was no one else in the apartment; and now seemed as good a time to act as any.

I did not purpose making any noise as I entered. Skor was armed and I was not, and it had been my intention to throw myself upon him from the rear and overpower him before he could have an opportunity to use his weapons against me. But the lock of the door clicked as I closed it, and Skor wheeled and faced me.

CHAPTER 17

In Hiding

As the eyes of the jong of Morov fell upon me he recognized me, and he voiced a sardonic laugh as he whipped out his sword and brought my charge to a sudden, ignominious stop – one does not finish a charge with the point of a sword in one's belly.

'So-o!' he exclaimed; 'it is you? Well, well! It is good to see you again. I did not expect to be so honored. I thought Fortune had been very kind to me when she returned the two young women. And now you have come! What a merry party we shall have!'

With the last words his tone, which had been sarcastically bantering, changed; he fairly hissed that gay sentence. And the expression on his face changed too. It became suddenly malevolent, and his eyes glittered with the same mad fire of insanity that I had seen there before.

Behind him stood Duare, her wide eyes fixed upon me with incredulity mixed with terror. 'Oh, why did you come, Carson!' she cried. 'Now he will kill you.'

'I will tell you why he came,' said Skor. 'He came for the other girl, for Nalte, not for you. You have been here a long time, but he did not come. Tonight one of my people seized the girl, Nalte, in Havatoo; and he came immediately to try to rescue her, the fool. I have known for a long time that they were in Havatoo. My spies have seen them there together. I do not know how he got here, but here he is – and here he stays, forever.'

He poked me in the belly with the point of his sword. 'How would you like to die, fool?' he demanded. 'A quick thrust through the heart perhaps. That would mutilate you least. You will make a fine specimen. Come now, what have you to say? Remember this will be the last chance you will have to think with your own brain; hereafter I shall do your thinking for you. You will sit in my banquet hall, and you will laugh when I tell you to laugh. You will see the two women who loved you, but they will shrink from the touch of your clammy hands, from your cold, dead lips. And whenever you see them, they will be with Skor in whose veins flows the bright blood of life.'

My plight seemed quite hopeless. The sword at my belly was slender, keen, and two-edged. I might have grasped it, but its edges were so sharp that it would have slipped through my fingers, severing them as it plunged into my body. Yet that I intended doing. I would not wait like a sheep the lethal blow of the butcher.

'You do not reply,' said Skor. 'Very well, we will have it over quickly!' He drew back his sword hand for the thrust.

Duare was standing just behind him beside a table littered with the sort of junk to which Skor seemed partial – his crazy *objets d'art*. I was waiting to seize the blade when he thrust. Skor hesitated a moment, I presumed to better enjoy my final agony; but in that he was disappointed. I would not give him that satisfaction; and so, to rob him of most of his pleasure, I laughed in his face.

At that moment Duare raised a heavy vase from the table, held it high above her, and crashed it down on Skor's head. Without a sound he shrank to the floor.

I leaped across his body to take Duare into my arms, but with a palm against my breast she pushed me away.

'Do not touch me!' she snapped. 'If you want to get out of Kormor, there is no time to be wasted. Come with me! I know where the girl you came to rescue is imprisoned.'

Her whole attitude toward me seemed to have changed, and my pride was piqued. In silence I followed her from the room. She led me into the corridor along which we had approached the room to which I had followed her and Skor. Opening a door at one side, she hurried along another corridor and stopped before a heavily bolted door.

'She is in here,' she said.

I drew the bolts and opened the door. Standing in the middle of the room beyond, looking straight at me, was Nalte. As she recognized me she gave a little cry of joy and, running toward me, threw her arms about me.

'Oh, Carson! Carson!' she cried. 'I knew that you would come; something told me that you would come.'

'We must hurry,' I told her. 'We must get out of here.'

I turned toward the door. Duare stood there, her chin in the air, her eyes flashing; but she said nothing. Nalte saw her then and recognized her. 'Oh, it is you!' she exclaimed.

'You are alive! I am so glad. We thought that you had been killed.'

Duare seemed puzzled by the evident sincerity of Nalte's manner, as though she had not expected that Nalte would be glad that she was alive. She softened a little. 'If we are to escape from Kormor, though I doubt that we can, we may not remain here,' she said. 'I think that I know a way out of the castle – a secret way that Skor uses. He showed me the door once during some strange mood of his insanity; but he has the key to the door on his person, and we must get that before we can do aught else.'

We returned to the room where we had left Skor's body, and as I entered it, I saw the jong of Morov stir and try to rise. He was not dead, though how he had survived that shattering blow I do not know. We had come just in time.

I ran toward him and threw him down. He was still only half conscious and made little or no resistance. I suppose I should have killed him, but I shrank from killing a defenseless man – even a fiend like Skor. Instead I bound and gagged him; then I searched him and found his keys.

After that Duare led us to the second floor of the palace and to a large room furnished in the bizarre taste that was Skor's. She crossed the apartment and drew aside a grotesque hanging, revealing a small door behind it.

'Here is the door,' she said; 'see if you can find a key to fit the lock.'

I tried several keys, and at last found the right one. The opened door revealed a narrow corridor which we entered after rearranging the hangings, and then closed the door behind us. A few steps brought us to the top of a spiral staircase. I went first, carrying Skor's sword which I had taken from him with his keys. The two girls followed closely behind me.

The stairway was lighted, for which I was glad, since it permitted us to move more rapidly and with greater safety. At the bottom was another corridor. I waited there until both girls stood beside me.

'Do you know where this corridor leads' I asked Duare.

'No,' she replied. 'All that Skor said was that he could get out of the castle this way without anyone seeing him – he always came and went this way. Practically everything that he did, the most commonplace things in life, he veiled with mystery and secrecy.'

'From the height of that stairway,' I said, 'I believe that we are below the ground level of the palace. I wish that we knew where this corridor ends, but there is only one way to find out. Come on!'

This corridor was but dimly illuminated by the light from the stairway, and the farther we went from the stairway the darker it became. It ran straight for a considerable distance, ending at the foot of a wooden stairway. Up this I groped my way only a few steps, when my head came in contact with a solid substance above me. I reached up and felt of the obstruction. It consisted of planking and was obviously a trap door. I tried to raise it, but could not. Then I searched around its edges with my fingers, and at last I found that which I sought – a latch. Tripping it, I pushed again; and the door gave. I opened it only an inch or two, but no light showed in the crack. Then I opened it wider and raised my head through the aperture.

Now I could see more, but not much more – only the dark interior of a room with a single small window through which the night light of Amtor showed dimly. Grasping the sword of the jong of Morov more tightly, I ascended the stairway and entered the room. I heard no sound.

The girls had followed me and now stood just behind me. I could hear them breathing. We stood waiting, listening. Slowly my eyes became accustomed to the darkness, and I made out what I thought was a door beside the single window. I crossed to it and felt; it was a door, but what lay beyond?

Cautiously I opened it and looked out into one of the sordid streets of Kormor. I looked about in an effort to orient myself and saw that the street was one of those that extended directly away from the palace which I could see looming darkly behind its wall at my right.

'Come!' I whispered, and with the girls behind me I stepped out into the street and turned to the left. 'If we meet any one,' I cautioned, 'remember to walk like the dead, shuffle along as you will see me do. Keep your eyes on the ground; it is our eyes that will most surely betray us.'

'Where are we going?' asked Duare in a whisper.

'I am going to try to find the house through which I came

into the city,' I replied, 'but I don't know that I can do so.'

'And if you can't?'

'Then we shall have to make an attempt to scale the city wall, but we shall find a way, Duare.'

'What difference will it make?' she murmured half to herself. 'If we escape from here, there will only be something else. I think I would rather be dead than go on any more.'

The note of hopelessness in her voice was so unlike Duare that it shocked me. 'You mustn't feel like that, Duare,' I expostulated. 'If we can get back to Havatoo, you will be safe and happy, and I have a surprise there for you that will give you new hope.' I was thinking of the plane in which we might hope to find Vepaja, the country that I could see she had about despaired of ever seeing again.

She shook her head. 'There is no hope, no hope of happiness, ever, for Duare.'

Some figures approaching us along the dusty street put an end to our conversation. With lowered eyes and shuffling feet we neared them. They passed, and I breathed again in relief.

It is useless to recount our futile search for the house I could not find. All the remainder of the night we searched, and with the coming of dawn I realized that we must find a place to hide until night came again.

I saw a house with a broken door, no unusual sight in dismal Kormor; and investigation indicated that it was tenantless. We entered and ascended to the second floor. Here, in a back room, we prepared to await the ending of the long day that lay ahead of us.

We were all tired, almost exhausted; and so we lay down on the rough planks and sought to sleep. We did not talk; each seemed occupied with his own dismal thoughts. Presently, from their regular breathing, I realized that the girls were both alseep; and very shortly thereafter I must have fallen asleep myself.

How long I slept I do not know. I was awakened by footsteps in an adjoining room. Some one was moving about, and I heard muttering as a person talking to himself.

Slowly I rose to my feet, holding Skor's sword in readiness. Its uselessness against the dead did not occur to me, yet had it I still would have felt safer with the sword in my hand.

The footsteps approached the door to the room in which we had sought sanctuary, and a moment later an old woman stopped upon the threshold and looked at me in wide-eyed astonishment.

'What are you doing here?' she demanded.

If she were surprised, no less was I; for old age was something I had never before seen in Amtor. Her voice awakened the girls, and I heard them rising to their feet behind me.

'What are you doing here?' repeated the old woman querulously. 'Get out of my house, accursed corpses! I'll have none of the spawn of Skor's evil brain in my house!'

I looked at her in astonishment. 'Aren't you dead?' I demanded.

'Of course I'm not dead!' she snapped.

'Neither are we,' I told her.

'Eh? Not dead?' She came closer. 'Let me see your eyes. No, they do not look like dead eyes; but they say that Skor has found some foul way in which to put a false light of life into dead eyes.'

'We are not dead,' I insisted.

'Then what are you doing in Kormor? I thought that I knew all of the living men and women here, and I do not know you. Are the women alive too?'

'Yes, we are all alive.' I thought quickly. I wondered if I might trust her with our secret and seek her aid. She evidently hated Skor, and we were already in her power if she wished to denounce us. I felt that we could not be much worse off in any event. 'We were prisoners of Skor. We escaped. We want to get out of the city. We are at your mercy. Will you help us, or will you turn us over to Skor to be murdered?'

'I won't turn you over to Skor,' she snapped. 'I wouldn't turn a dead mistal over to that fiend; but I don't know how I can help you. You can't get out of Kormor. The dead sentries along the wall never sleep.'

'I got into Kormor without being seen by a sentry,' I said. 'If I could only find the house, I could get out again.'

'What house?' she demanded.

'The house at the end of the tunnel that runs under Gerlat kum Rov to Havatoo.'

'A tunnel to Havatoo! I never heard of such a thing. Are you sure?'

'I came through it last night,' I assured her.

She shook her head. 'Well, I don't know where it is; but I'll help you. At least I can hide you and give you food. We always help one another here in Kormor, we who are alive.'

'There are other living people in Kormor?' I asked.

'A few,' she replied. 'Skor has not succeeded in hunting us all out yet. We live a mean life, always hiding; but it is life. If he found us, he would make us like those others.'

She came closer. 'I cannot believe you are alive,' she said. 'Perhaps you are tricking me.' She touched my face, and then ran her palms over the upper part of my body. 'You are warm,' she said, and then she felt my pulse. 'Yes, you are alive.'

Similarly she examined Duare and Nalte, and at last she was convinced that we had told her the truth. 'Come,' she said, 'I will take you to a better place than this. You will be more comfortable. I do not use this house very often.'

She led us downstairs and out into a yard at the rear of which stood another house. It was a mean house, poorly furnished. She took us into a back room and told us to remain there.

'I suppose you want food,' she said.

'And water,' added Nalte; 'I have had none since yesterday evening.'

'You poor thing,' said the old woman. 'I'll get it for you. How young and pretty you are! Once I was young and pretty too.'

'Why have you aged?' I asked. 'I thought that all the people of Amtor held the secret of longevity.'

'Aye, but how may one obtain the serum in Kormor? We had it once, before Skor came; but he took it away from us. He said that he would create a new race that would not require it, for they would never grow old. The effects of my last inoculation have worn off, and now I am growing old and shall die. It is not so bad to die – if Skor does not find one's corpse. We of the living here bury our dead in secret beneath the floors of our houses. My mate and our two children lie beneath this floor. But I must go and fetch food and water for you. I shall not be gone long,' and with that, she left us.

'Poor old creature,' said Nalte. 'She has nothing to which to look forward except the grave, and with the chance that Skor may rob her of that poor future.'

'How strange she looked!' there was a shocked expression in Duare's eyes as she spoke. 'So that is old age! I never saw it before. That is the way I should look some day, were it not for the serum! How ghastly! Oh, I should rather die than be like that. Old age! Oh, how terrible!'

Here was a unique experience. I was witnessing the reactions of a nineteen-year-old girl who had never before seen the ravages of old age, and I could not but wonder if the subconscious effect of old age on youth accustomed to seeing it were not similar. But these meditations were interrupted by the return of the old woman, and with it I caught a new insight into the character of Duare.

As the old woman entered the room, her arms laden, Duare ran forward and took the things from her. 'You should have let me come with you and help you,' she said. 'I am younger and stronger.'

Then she placed the food and water upon a table, and with a sweet smile she put an arm about the withered shoulders of the old crone and drew her toward a bench. 'Sit down,' she said. 'Nalte and I will prepare the food. You just sit here and rest until it is ready, and then we shall all eat together.'

The old woman looked at her in astonishment for a moment and then burst into tears. Duare dropped to the bench beside her and put her arms about her. 'Why do you cry?' she asked.

'I don't know why I cry,' sobbed the old creature. 'I feel like singing, but I cry. It has been so long since I have heard kind words, since any one has cared whether I were happy or sad, tired or rested.'

I saw the tears come to Duare's eyes and to Nalte's, and they had to busy themselves with the preparation of the food to hide their emotions.

That night a dozen of the living of Kormor came to the house of Kroona, the old woman who had befriended us. They were all very old, some of them older than Kroona. They laughed at Kroona's fears that Skor wanted them; and pointed out, as evidently they had many times before, that if it were old bodies Skor wanted, he long since could have found them, for their old age was ample evidence that they were of the living. But Kroona insisted that they were all in danger; and I soon realized that it was her pet obsession, without which she would probably be more miserable than she was with it. She got a great thrill out of leading a life of constant danger and hiding first in one house and then in another.

But they were all of one opinion that we were in great danger, and the dear old things pledged themselves to help us in every way they could – to bring us food and water and hide us from our enemies. That was all that they could do, for none of them believed that it were possible to escape from Kormor – such is the hopelessness of old age.

Early the following morning a very old man, one of the visitors of the previous evening, hobbled into the house. He was perturbed and greatly excited. His palsied hands were trembling. 'They are searching the city for you,' he whispered. 'There is a terrible story of what you did to Skor and of what Skor will do to you when he finds you. All night and all day and all last night he lay bound and helpless where you left him; then one of his creatures found and released him. Now the whole city is being scoured for you. They may be here any minute.'

'What can we do?' asked Duare. 'Where can we hide?'

'You can do nothing,' said the old man, 'but wait until they come. There is no place in all Kormor that they will not search.'

'We can do something,' said Nalte; then she turned to our informant. 'Can you get us paints such as the corpses use to make themselves appear like living men?'

'Yes,' said the old man.

'Well, go quickly and fetch them,' urged Nalte.

The old man hobbled out of the room, mumbling to himself.

'It is the only way, Nalte,' I cried. 'I believe that if he returns in time we can fool them; dead men are not very bright.'

It seemed a long time before the old man came back; but he came finally, and he brought a large box of make-up with him. It was quite an elaborate affair which he said that he had obtained from a friend of his, a living man, whose craft was applying the make-up to corpses.

Quickly Nalte went to work on Duare and soon had transformed her into an old woman with lines and wrinkles and hollows. The hair was the most difficult problem to solve, but we finally succeeded in approximating the results we desired, though we used up all of the cosmeticians' white pigment, rubbing it into our hair.

Duare and I together worked on Nalte, for we knew that we had no time to spare, the old man having brought word when he returned with the make-up that the searchers were working in the next block and coming our way; then Nalte and Duare transformed me into a very sad-looking old man.

Kroona said that we should each have some task that we could be performing when the searchers arrived, so that we might appear natural. She gave Duare and Nalte some old rags which they might pretend to be fashioning into garments, and she sent me out into the yard to dig a hole. It was fortunate that she did so, because the association of ideas resulting reminded me that I must hide Skor's sword. Were that found we were doomed.

I wrapped it up in a piece of cloth and carried it out in the yard with me, and you may take my word for it that I dug one hole there in record time. When I had covered the sword with dirt, I started digging another hole beside it and threw that dirt also on the spot above the weapon.

I had just finished when the yard gate was thrown open and a score of dead men came shuffling in. 'We are looking for the strangers who escaped from the palace,' said one. 'Are they here?'

I cupped my hand behind my ear and said, 'Eh?'

The fellow repeated his question, shouting very loud and again I did the same thing and said, 'Eh?' Then he gave up and went on into the house, followed by the others.

I heard them searching in there, and every instant I expected to hear cries of excitement when one of them discovered and pierced the thin disguises of Duare or Nalte.

CHAPTER 18

UNDER SUSPICION

SKOR'S creatures searched Kroona's house far more carefully than they would have searched that of one of their own kind, for Skor must have assumed that of all the people in Kormor the living would be most likely to aid the living; but at last they came out and went away. And I sat down on the pile of dirt I had dug and mopped the perspiration from my forehead, nor was it the sweat of toil. I think that for fifteen minutes I had come as near to sweating blood as a man can.

When I went into the house I found Duare, Nalte, and Kroona just sitting there in dazed silence. They couldn't seem to realize that we had passed through the ordeal successfully.

'Well,' I said, 'that's over.'

My voice seemed to break the spell, and they all stirred.

'Do you know what saved us?' demanded Nalte.

'Why, our disguises of course,' I replied.

'Yes,' she admitted, 'they helped, but our real salvation was the stupidity of the searchers. They scarcely looked at us. They were hunting for somebody who was *hidden*, and because we were not hiding they didn't give us a second thought.'

'Do you think we might remove the paint now?' asked Duare. 'It is very uncomfortable.'

'I think we should not remove it at all,' I replied. 'As we know, they won't find us in this search; so Skor may order another search, and next time we may not have time to disguise ourselves even if we are lucky enough to get the materials again.'

'I suppose you are right,' said Duare, 'and after all the discomfort is not much by comparison with what we have already gone through.'

'The disguises have one advantage,' said Nalte. 'We can move about more freely without danger of detection. We won't have to sit in this stuffy little back room all the time, and I for one am going to the front of the house and get a breath of fresh air.'

It was not a bad suggestion, and Duare and I joined Nalte while Kroona went about some household duties. The front room on the second floor, to which we went, overlooked the street. We could hear the searchers ransacking the house next door, and we could see the pedestrians shuffling along the dusty street.

Suddenly Nalte seized my arm and pointed. 'See that man?' she exclaimed in an excited whisper.

Shuffling along the street was a large corpse painted in the semblance of life. His trappings were finer than those ordinarily seen in Kormor. Only his peculiar gait revealed to the initiated eye the fact that he was not as alive as we that Death was masquerading as Life.

'Yes, I see him,' I replied. 'What about him?'

'He is the man that abducted me from Havatoo!'

'Are you sure?' I demanded.

'Absolutely,' replied Nalte. 'As long as I live I shall never forget that face.'

A plan, perhaps I had better call it an inspiration, shot into my mind. 'I am going to follow him,' I said. 'I shall be back soon. Hope for the best,' and then I turned and hurried from the room.

A moment later I was in the street. The fellow was only a short distance ahead of me as I turned into the street. If my guess were correct, he would lead me eventually to the entrance to the tunnel that leads to Havatoo. Perhaps not today, but if I learned where he lived today, then some other day.

His gait was more rapid than that of the average Kormoran, and he walked as though with a definite purpose in view. I judged that he was one of Skor's more successful experiments, and that for this reason he had been chosen as one of the jong's agents in Havatoo, where the ordinary run of Kormoran corpses could not long have passed themselves off as living men.

As I followed him I noted carefully every detail of the street in which we were; so that I would not again be unable to return to my starting point. When presently he turned into a street leading toward the river my hopes rose, and I noted carefully the buildings at the inter-section.

Near the river the fellow turned into a small alley, followed it to the next street, and then turned again toward the river. Directly ahead of us, even before he turned into it, I saw and recognized the building beneath which lay the Kormor end of the tunnel.

At the gateway leading into the yard before the house the man turned for the first time and looked behind him, I presume to see if he were being observed. Then he saw me.

There was nothing for me to do but keep on toward him. I kept my eyes on the ground and paid no attention to him as I approached him, though I could almost feel his gaze upon me. It seemed an eternity before I reached him. I was about to breathe a sigh of relief as I passed him, and then he spoke to me.

'Who are you, and what are you doing here?' he demanded.

'I am looking for another house to live in,' I cackled. 'The doors and the windows have all fallen off mine.'

'There are no houses here for you,' he snapped. 'Your kind is not allowed in this district. Get out of here, and never let me see you here again.'

'Yes,' I replied meekly, and turned back.

To my great joy he let me go, and a moment later I had turned into the alley and was hidden from his view. But I had learned what I wanted to know, and my blood was tingling with happiness. Now only the worst of ill fortune could prevent my guiding Duare and Nalte back to the safety of Havatoo.

As I made my way through the streets of Kormor toward the house of Kroona, my mind was filled with thoughts and plans for escape. I was determined to leave as soon as darkness fell, and already I was looking forward to and planning on what I should do upon my return to Havatoo.

As I entered Kroona's house I saw immediately, even before any one had a chance to speak, that something was amiss. Duare and Nalte both rushed toward me, and it was evident that both were perturbed. Kroona and the old man who had brought us the pigments with which we had disguised ourselves were cackling together excitedly.

'At last you are back!' cried Nalte. 'We thought that you would never come.'

'Perhaps it is not too late even now,' said Duare.

'I wanted them to come with me and let me hide them,' croaked Kroona, 'but neither one of them would leave without you. They said that if you were to be taken, then they would be taken too.'

'What in the world are you all talking about?' I demanded. 'What has happened? I can't make head nor tail of it.'

'It is soon told,' said the old man who had brought us the make-up. 'The cosmetician from whom I borrowed the materials to change you into old people has betrayed us in order to curry favour with Skor. A man heard him tell his servant to go to the palace and inform Skor that he would lead Skor's men to this hiding place of yours. The man was a friend of mine and came and told me. Skor's men may be here any minute now.'

I thought rapidly; then I turned to Duare and Nalte. 'Get your make-up off as quickly as you can,' I directed, 'and I will do the same.'

'But then we shall be lost for certain,' exclaimed Duare.

'On the contrary,' I replied, as I commenced to remove the pigment from my blond head.

'They will know us at once without our disguise,' insisted Duare, but I was glad to see that both she and Nalte were following my example and removing the paint from their hair and faces.

'Our own youth will be the best disguise we can adopt in this emergency,' I explained. 'These creatures of Skor are none too intelligent, and having been sent to find three fugitives who have disguised themselves as very old people they will be looking only for those who appear very old. If we can get out of the house before they come, I think that we shall have a good chance to avoid detection.'

We worked rapidly and soon had the last vestiges of our disguises removed; then we thanked Kroona and the old man, bid them good-bye, and left the house. As we entered the street, we saw a body of warriors approaching from the direction of the palace.

'We were not quite in time,' said Nalte. 'Shall we turn and run for it?'

'No,' I replied. 'That would only arouse their suspicions immediately, and they would pursue and most certainly overtake us. Come! We shall go and meet them.'

'What!' demanded Duare in astonishment. 'Are we going to give ourselves up?'

'By no means,' I replied. 'We are going to take a great chance, but there is no alternative. If they see three people walking away from them, they will investigate, and if they do that, we may be recognized; but if they see us approaching them, they will believe that we do not fear anything from them and will be convinced therefore that we are not those whom they seek. Walk with the shuffling gait of the dead, and keep your eyes on the ground. Duare, you walk ahead, Nalte a few paces behind you; I shall cross to the other side of the street. By separating we shall attract less attention; they are looking for three people whom they expect to find together.'

'I hope that your reasoning is correct,' said Duare, but it was evident that she was skeptical. I was none too enthusiastic about the plan myself, but I could think of no other.

I crossed the street which happened to be the side along which the warriors were approaching; in fact I had chosen it for that reason. knowing that there was less likelihood that any of them would recognize me than that they would know Duare who had been in Skor's palace for some time.

I must admit that I felt none too comfortable as the distance between me and the warriors steadily lessened, but I kept my eyes on the ground and shuffled slowly along.

As I came abreast of them their leader halted and addressed me. My heart stood still. 'Where is the house of Kroona?' he asked.

'I do not know,' I replied and shuffled on my way. Momentarily I expected to be seized, but the warriors went on their way and let me go on mine. My ruse had been successful!

As soon as I felt that it was safe, I crossed to the opposite side of the street, and as I caught up with the two girls, I told them to follow behind me but not too closely.

It still lacked an hour until sunset, and I did not dare risk approaching the entrance to the tunnel until after dark.

In the meantime we must find a place to hide and keep off the streets where every moment we were in danger of arousing suspicion.

Turning into a side street, I soon found a deserted house,

of which there are many in Kormor; and presently we were in hiding again.

Both girls were dejected. I could tell by their silence and listlessness. The future must have seemed hopeless to them, yet they voiced no complaints.

'I have some good news for you,' I said.

Duare looked at me with scarcely any indication of interest, as though there never could be any good news for her again. She had been unusually silent since our escape from the palace. She seldom spoke unless directly addressed; and she avoided speech with Nalte as much as possible, although her manner toward her was not definitely unfriendly.

'What is the good news?' demanded Nalte. 'I was commencing to give up hope.'

'I have found the entrance to the tunnel to Havatoo,' I replied.

The effect of that statement upon Nalte was electrical, but it seemed to arouse only passive interest in Duare. 'In Havatoo,' she said, 'I shall be as far as ever from Vepaja.'

'But your life will not be in danger,' I reminded her.

She shrugged. 'I do not know that I care to live,' she replied.

'Don't be discouraged, Duare,' I begged. 'Once we are in Havatoo I am confident that I shall discover a way to find Vepaja and return you to your people.' I was thinking of the plane ready and waiting in its hangar on Kantum Lat, but I didn't say anything about it. I wanted to save it as a surprise for her; and, anyway, we were not yet in Havatoo.

The two hours that we waited until complete darkness enveloped the city were as long a two hours as I have ever spent; but at last is seemed safe to attempt to reach the silent, deserted house near the river front, where all our hopes were centred.

The street was deserted when we left the building where we had been hiding, I was certain of my way to our destination, and without delay or adventure we at last came in sight of the decaying structure that hid the entrance to our avenue of escape.

I led the girls into the dark interior of the building, and there we huddled in the dark, listening. I regretted then that I had been unable to retrieve the sword that I had taken from Skor and buried in the yard of Kroona's home. It would have given me a feeling of far greater security than I now enjoyed.

Satisfied at last that we werc the sole occupants of the building and that no one had followed us, I crossed to the doorway that hid the entrance to the tunnel, Duare and Nalte close behind me.

I had no difficulty in finding the latch, and a moment later we were descending into the dark corridor with liberty and safety almost in our grasp.

There was a chance that we might meet one of Skor's creatures returning from Havatoo; but I felt that everything was in our favour inasmuch as one of them had just crossed in the opposite direction, and there had never been any evidence that they were in Havatoo in great numbers. It was my opinion that the two that set upon Nalte and me were alone in that venture, and if that were true, it was also doubtless true that Skor never had more than a couple of his retainers in Havatoo at the same time. I certainly hoped that I was right.

In silence, through the utter darkness, we groped our way along the cold, moist corridor beneath the River of Death. I moved more rapidly than I had when I had come through it to Kormor, for I knew now that no pitfalls lay in my path.

At last I felt the stairs leading upward at the tunnel's end, and a moment later I stopped behind the door that would let us into Havatoo. I did not wait; I did not listen. Nothing could have stopped me then. I would have grappled a dozen of the gruesome corpses of Kormor had they stood in my way, and I believe that I should have overcome them so desperate was I.

But I met neither dead nor living as we stepped out onto the lower floor of the dismal building off the Havatoo Lat. Quickly we crossed to the front of the building and out through the door there to the street beyond, and a moment later we stood in the Havatoo Lat with its brilliant lights and its two streams of traffic.

We were a conspicuous trio in our mean garments of rags with which we had sought to disguise ourselves in Kormor, and many were the suspicious glances cast in our direction.

As quickly as I could I hailed a public conveyance and

instructed the driver to take us to the home of Ero Shan, and as we settled down upon the cushions we relaxed for the first time in many a day.

We talked a great deal during the drive, particularly Nalte and I. Duare was very quiet. She spoke of the beauty of Havatoo and the wonders that surrounded us, all strange and new to her, but only briefly and then lapsed into silence again.

Our driver had eyed us suspiciously when we entered his car, and when he deposited us in front of the house of Ero Shan he behaved peculiarly.

But Ero Shan was delighted to see us. He ordered food and drink, and plied us with questions until he had had the whole story from us several times. He congratulated me upon finding Duare, but I could see that his greatest happiness lay in the return of Nalte. His eyes devoured her.

The girls were tired and needed rest, and we were preparing to take them to Nalte's home when the first blow fell that was to put the lives of two of us in jeopardy and plunge us all from the heights of happiness to the depths of despair.

There was a summons at the main entrance, and presently a servant entered the room. Behind him was a file of warriors commanded by an officer.

Ero Shan looked up in surprise. He knew the officer and called him by name, asking him what brought him here with armed men.

'I am sorry, Ero Shan,' the man replied, 'but I have orders from the Sanjong itself to arrest three suspicious appearing people who were seen to enter your house earlier in the evening.'

'But,' exclaimed Ero Shan, 'no one has entered my house but Carson Napier, whom you know, and these two young women. They are all my friends.'

The officer was eyeing our mean apparel and evidently not without suspicion. 'These must be those I was sent to arrest if no one else has entered your house this evening,' he said.

There was nothing to do but accompany the warriors, and this we did. Ero Shan came with us, and a short time later we were before an investigating board of three men.

The complaining witness was the driver who had brought us from the house that hid the entrance to the tunnel to

Ero Shan's. He said that he lived in the neighborhood, and having known of the abduction of Nalte, he was immediately suspicious when he saw three people, garbed as we were, in the vicinity of the place.

He accused us of being spies from Kormor and insisted that we were but painted corpses like the man I had grappled with at the time of the abduction of Nalte.

The examining board listened to my story; then they examined Nalte and Duare briefly. They questioned Ero Shan concerning us, and without leaving the room they discharged Nalte and myself and ordered Duare back for a further examination by the official examining board the following day.

I thought that they seemed a little suspicious of Duare; and so did Ero Shan, though he only admitted this after we had returned the girls to Nalte's home and were alone.

'Justice sometimes miscarries in Havatoo,' he said gravely. 'The loathing that we feel for Kormor and everything connected with it colors all our decisions in matters concerning it. Duare admits having been in Kormor for some time. She admits having resided in the palace of Skor, the jong. The examining board knows nothing about her other than what she claims and what you tell them, but they do not know that they can believe either of you. You will recall that the result of your examination was not such as to create considerable confidence in you.'

'And you think that Duare may be in danger?' I asked.

'I cannot tell,' he replied. 'Everything may come out all right; but, on the other hand, if the board has the slightest suspicion concerning Duare, it will order her destroyed, for our theory of justice is that it is better to do an injustice to a single individual than to risk the safety and welfare of many. Sometimes that policy is a cruel one, but results have demonstrated that it is better for the race than a policy of weak sentimentalism.'

I did not sleep well that night. The weight of a great fear for the outcome of tomorrow's trial oppressed me.

CHAPTER 19

Flight

I was not permitted to accompany Duare to her examination. She was placed in charge of the same woman who had guarded Nalte at the time of her examination, Hara Es.

To pass the hours until the result should be made known, I went to the hangar to inspect my plane. It was in perfect condition. The motor hummed almost noiselessly. I could not, under ordinary circumstances, have withstood the urge to have the ship wheeled out onto the plain before the city for a trial flight; but my mind was so distraught with apprehension concerning the fate of Duare that I had no heart for anything.

I spent an hour alone in the hangar. None of my assistants was there, they having all returned to their ordinary duties after the completion of the plane. Then I returned to the house that I shared with Ero Shan.

He was not there. I tried to read, but I could not concentrate long enough to know what I was reading about. My eyes followed the strange Amtorian characters, but my thoughts were with Duare. At last I gave it up and walked in the garden. An unreasoning terror enveloped me like a shroud, numbing my faculties.

How long I walked I do not know, but at last my sad reveries were interrupted by the approach of footsteps through the house. I knew that Ero Shan must be coming to the garden. I stood waiting, looking toward the doorway through which he must come; and the instant that I saw him my heart turned cold. I read the confirmation of my worst fears in the expression on his face.

He came and laid a hand upon my shoulder. 'I have bad news for you, my friend,' he said.

'I know,' I replied; 'I read it in your eyes. They have ordered her destroyed?'

'It is a miscarriage of justice,' he said, 'but there is no appeal. We must accept the decision as the board's honest conviction that they are thus serving the best interests of the city.'

'Is there nothing I can do?' I asked.

'Nothing,' he replied.

'Won't they let me take her away from Havatoo?'

'No; they are so afraid of the contaminating influence of Skor and his creatures that they will never permit one to live that falls into their hands.'

'But she is not one of Skor's creatures!' I insisted.

'I am quite sure that they had their doubts, but the benefit of the doubt is given to the city and not to the accused. There is nothing more to be done.'

'Do you think they would let me see her?' I asked.

'It is possible,' he replied. 'For some reason she is not to be destroyed until tomorrow.'

'Will you try to arrange it for me, Ero Shan?'

'Certainly,' he replied. 'Wait here, and I will see what I can do.'

I have never spent such long and bitter hours as those while I was awaiting the return of Ero Shan. Never before had I felt so helpless and hopeless in the face of an emergency. Had these been ordinary men with whom I had to deal, I might have seen somewhere a ray of hope; but there was none here. Their uprightness precluded the possibility that I might influence even a minor guard by bribery; they could not be moved by an appeal to sentiment; the cold, hard logic of their reasoning left their minds impregnable fortresses of conviction that it were useless to assail.

I have said that I was hopeless, but that was not entirely true. Upon what my hope fed I do not know, but it seemed so impossible to believe that Duare was to be destroyed that my mind must in some slight measure have been stunned.

It was dark before Ero Shan returned. I could read neither hope nor despair in his expression as he entered the room where I had finally gone to await him. He appeared very serious and very tired.

'Well?' I demanded. 'What is the verdict? Were you successful?'

'I had a hard time of it,' he said. 'I had to go all the way up to the Sanjong, but at last I got permission for you to visit her.'

'Where is she? When may I see her?'

'I will take you to her now,' he replied.

After we entered his car I asked him how he accomplished it.

'I finally took Nalte with me,' he replied. 'She knew more about you and all that you and Duare have passed through together than any one else in Havatoo. For a while I almost thought that she was going to persuade the Sanjong to reverse the verdict against Duare, and it was solely through her appeal that they at last gave their consent to this last meeting.

'I learned a great deal about you and Duare from Nalte, much more than you have ever told me; and I learned something else.'

'What was that?' I asked as he paused.

'I learned that I love Nalte,' he replied.

'And did you learn that she loves you?'

'Yes. Were it not for your unhappiness, I should be quite the happiest man in Havatoo tonight. But what made you think that Nalte loved me?'

'She told me so.'

'And you did not tell me?' he asked reproachfully.

'I could not,' I replied, 'until after I knew that you loved her.'

'I suppose not. She told me that you were planning on taking her back to Andoo; but now that won't be necessary – she seems quite content to remain in Havatoo.'

We had been driving along the Korgan Lat toward the stadium, and now Ero Shan turned into a side street and stopped before a small house.

'Here we are,' he said. 'This is the house of Hara Es, in whose charge Duare has been placed. Hara Es is expecting you. I shall wait out here. You are to be allowed to remain with Duare for five vir.'

Five vir are a little over twenty minutes of earth time. It seemed all too short, but it was better than nothing. I went to the door of the house, and in answer to my summons Hara Es admitted me.

'I have been expecting you,' she said. 'Come with me.'

She led me up to the second floor and unlocking a door, pushed it open. 'Go in,' she directed. 'In five vir I shall come for you.'

As I entered the room Duare rose from a couch and faced me. Hara Es closed the door and locked it. I heard her footsteps as she descended the stairs. We were alone, Duare and I, for the first time in what seemed an eternity.

'Why did you come here?' asked Duare in a tired voice.

'You ask me that!' I exclaimed. 'You know why I came.'

She shook her head. 'You cannot do anything for me; no one can. I suppose you would come if you could help me, but as you can't, I do not know why you came.'

'If for no other reason, because I love you. Is not that reason enough?'

'Do not speak to me of love. I am about to die, but I am still the daughter of a jong of Vepaja.'

Even in this last extremity Duare remained a victim of the foolish restrictions imposed upon her by her royal blood, and I determined not to make her last moments more unhappy by pressing unwelcome attentions upon her, although it was only with the greatest difficulty that I refrained from taking her in my arms and covering those beautiful lips with kisses.

I sought to cheer her, but she said that she was not unhappy.

'I am not afraid to die, Carson Napier,' she said. 'As it seems impossible that living, I should ever return to Vepaja, I prefer to die. I am not happy. I can never be happy. It is better then that I die.'

'Why could you never be happy?' I demanded.

'That is my secret; I shall take it to the grave with me. Let us not speak of it any more.'

'I don't wish you to die, Duare. You must not die!' I exclaimed.

'I know that you feel that way, Carson, but what are we to do about it?'

'There must be something we can do. How many are there in this house beside Hara Es and yourself?'

'There is no one.'

Suddenly a mad hope possessed me. I searched the room with my eyes. It was bare of all except absolute necessities. I saw nothing with which I might carry out my plan. Time was flying. Hara Es would soon return. My eyes fell upon the saronglike scarf that Duare wore, the common outer garment of Amtorian women.

'Let me take this, I said, stepping to her side.

'What for?' she demanded.

'Never mind. Do as I say! We have no time to argue.'

Duare had long since learned to submerge her pride when my tone told her that an emergency confronted us and to obey me promptly. She did so now. Quickly she unwound the scarf from about her and handed it to me.

'Here it is,' she said. 'What are you going to do with it?'

'Wait and see. Stand over there on the right side of the room. Here comes Hara Es now; I hear her on the stairs.'

I stepped quickly to one side of the door so that I should be behind it and hidden from Hara Es as she entered. Then I waited. More than my own life lay in the balance, yet I was not nervous. My heart beat as quietly as though I were contemplating nothing more exciting than a pleasant social visit.

I heard Hara Es stop before the door. I heard the key turn in the lock. Then the door swung open and Hara Es stepped into the room. As she did so I seized her by the throat from behind and pushed the door shut with my foot.

'Don't make a sound,' I warned, 'or I shall have to kill you.'

She did not lose her poise for an instant. 'You are very foolish,' she said. 'This will not save Duare, and it will mean your death. You cannot escape from Havatoo.'

I made no reply, but worked quickly and in silence. I bound her securely with the scarf and then gagged her. When I had finished, I raised her from the floor and laid her on the couch.

'I am sorry, Hara Es, for what I was compelled to do. I am going now to get rid of Ero Shan. He will know nothing of what I have done. Please be sure to inform the Sanjong that Ero Shan is in no way responsible for what has happened – or what is going to happen. I shall leave you here until I can get away from Ero Shan without arousing his suspicions.

'In the mean time, Duare, watch Hara Es closely until I return. See that she does not loosen her bonds.'

I stooped and picked the key from the floor where Hara Es had dropped it; then I quit the room, locking the door after me. A moment later I was in the car with Ero Shan.

'Let's get home as quickly as possible,' I said; then I lapsed into silence, a silence which Ero Shan, respecting what he thought to be my sorrow, did not break.

He drove rapidly, but it seemed an eternity before he drove the car into the garage at the house. There being no thieves in Havatoo locks are unnecessary; so our garage doors stood wide open as they always were except in inclement weather. My car, facing toward the street, stood beside Ero Shan's.

'You have eaten scarcely anything all day,' said Ero Shan as we entered the house; 'suppose we have something now.'

'No, thanks,' I replied. 'I am going to my room. I could not eat now.'

He laid a hand upon my arm and pressed it gently, but he did not say anything; then he turned and left me. A wonderful friend was Ero Shan. I hated to deceive him, but I would have deceived my God to save Duare.

I went to my room, but only long enough to procure weapons; then I returned to the garage. As I stepped into my car, I offered a prayer of thanks that the motors of Havatoo are silent. Like a wraith the car slipped out of the garage into the night, and as I passed the house I whispered a silent good-bye to Ero Shan.

Approaching the house of Hara Es, I felt the first qualm of nervousness that had assailed me during this adventure, but the house seemed quite deserted as I entered it and ran up the stairs to the second floor.

Unlocking the door of the room in which I had left Duare and Hara Es, I breathed a sigh of relief as I saw them both there. I crossed quickly to the couch and examined Hara Es's bonds. They appeared quite secure.

'Come!' I said to Duare. 'We have no time to waste.'

She followed me out of the room, I locked the door on Hara Es, found another sarong for Duare in a room on the first floor, and a moment later Duare and I were in my car.

'Where are we going?' she asked. 'We cannot hide in Havatoo. They will find us.'

'We are going to leave Havatoo for ever,' I replied, and just then I saw a car pass us and draw up in front of the house we had just left. Two men were in it; one of them jumped out and ran to the door; then I opened the throttle. I had seen enough to turn me cold with apprehension.

Duare had seen, too. 'Now they will discover everything,' she said, 'and you will be killed. I knew that it would end in disaster. Oh, why didn't you let me die alone? I want to die.'

'But I won't let you!'

She said nothing more, and we sped through the now almost deserted streets of Havatoo toward the Kantum Lat and the Gate of the Physicists.

We had gone about two miles of the three that we must cover before we reached our destination when I heard an ominous sound such as I had never before heard in Havatoo. It sounded like the wailing of sirens such as are used on police cars in the large cities of America. Instantly I knew that it was an alarm, and I guessed that the man who had entered the house of Hara Es had discovered her and that our escape was known.

Closer and closer came the sounds of the wailing sirens as I drew up before the hangar where my plane stood; they seemed to be converging upon us from all directions. I was not surprised that they should have guessed where they would find us, for it would have been obvious to even duller minds than those of Havatoo that here lay my only chance to escape.

Fairly dragging Duare with me, I leaped from the car and ran into the hangar. The great doors, operated by mechanical means, rolled open to the touch of a button. I lifted Duare into the cockpit. She asked no questions; there was no time for questions.

Then I took my place at her side. I had designed the plane for training purposes; and it had two seats, each accommodating two people. I started the motor – and such a motor! Silent, vibrationless, and it required no warming up.

I taxied out into the Kantum Lat. The sirens were very close now. I saw the lights of cars tearing down upon us. As I started toward the Gate of the Physicists I heard the staccato hum of Amtorian rifles behind us. They were firing at us!

I nosed up; the wheels left the ground; the great gate loomed directly ahead. Up! Faster! Faster! I held my breath. Would we make it? Responding perfectly, the light ship climbed almost vertically in the last few seconds; she sped over the top of the lofty gate with only inches to spare. We were safe!

CONCLUSION

FAR below, the lights of Havatoo lay behind us as I turned the ship's nose toward the shimmering ribbon that was the River of Death, the River of Life, to us, that was to guide us down to that unknown sea where, perchance, we might find Vepaja.

Duare had not spoken. I felt her arm against mine trembling. I reached over and laid a hand upon it. 'Why are you trembling?' I asked. 'You are quite safe now.'

'What is this thing we are in?' she asked. 'Why does it not fall to the ground and kill us? What keeps it up.?'

I explained as best I could, telling her that there was no danger that it would fall; and then she drew a deep, long sigh of relief.

'If you say that we are safe; then I am afraid no longer,' she said. 'But tell me, why are you making this sacrifice for me?'

'What sacrifice?' I asked.

'You can never return to Havatoo now; they would kill you.'

'I do not want to return to Havatoo if you cannot live there in safety,' I replied.

'But what of Nalte?' she asked. 'You love one another, and now you can never see her again.'

'I do not love Nalte, nor does she love me. I love only you, Duare; and Nalte and Ero Shan love one another.'

She sat in silence for a long time; then, presently, she turned and looked up into my face. 'Carson!' she said in a low voice.

'Yes, Duare, what is it?'

'I love you!'

I could not believe that I had heard aright. 'But, Duare, you are the daughter of a jong of Vepaja!' I exclaimed.

'That I have known always,' she said, 'but I have just learned that before that I am a woman.'

I took her in my arms then. I could have held her thus forever, but I had to release her a moment later to right the ship as it went into a tail spin.

THE END